Speak for the Dead
The Reaper's Son Book 1
Catherine Kruta

Copyright © 2025 Catherine Kruta

Content Warnings: Mentions of sexual assault, child death, animal death

First paperback edition November 2025
Cover art by Jovanna Plata
ISBN 979-8-9998027-0-5 (paperback)
ISBN 979-8-9998027-1-2 (ebook)
The Solo Geographer
www.catherinekruta.com

For my cousin and fellow book worm Blythe Leer
who never got to hold this book in her hands.

CHAPTER ONE

The dead girl's soul stared at him, her eyes a blank space in her ghostly pale face. She stood at the head of her body, splayed on the cold pavement of the alley. She couldn't speak. Patrick ducked under the crime scene tape and looked over his shoulder. The officers were questioning the café owner that found her. Finding a dead body on the street at 7:00 AM was very unusual for the Central West End. Well, finding a dead body at any time of day was very unusual for the Central West End. The girl's white shirt was ripped open, her bra cut between her breasts, her black skirt pushed up around her waist, and her shoes were missing. He could see no visible signs of injury, which was concerning. Faded bruises peppered her bare legs. Her arms were tied under her body with her own tights, and her head bent to the left, her dyed black hair covering her face. He knelt down next to her.

"Schneider found her about half an hour ago."

Patrick looked up at the voice. He hadn't even noticed Detective Beck was at the crime scene already. In spite of his good looks, he looked like hell. His eyes were red, and he had stubble on his jaw. It was an increasingly common look for the detective. "Haven't seen you here in a while," Patrick said as he turned back to the body.

Beck chuckled and knelt beside the body across from Patrick. "I work all over the county now," he said. "Ever since Julie was posted here a couple months ago."

Patrick didn't ask for elaboration. He didn't much care about the FBI's presence in the city's investigations. "Schneider, the owner of the café?" he asked.

Beck nodded. Patrick looked up and down the body, ignoring the soul. She couldn't speak. They never could. "He said she wasn't there when his baker came in at 3 AM. So she had to have been dropped between then and 6:30. We've already gotten several pictures of the body."

1

Patrick put on a pair of gloves and pushed the hair out of her face. The skin was pristine. Her eyes were open, revealing startling ice-blue irises. "No marks on her neck." He shook his head. "It's difficult to say how she died. I can't see any visible trauma. No bruising."

"Her clothing and positioning indicate sexual assault," Beck continued. "We couldn't find any sort of ID, but CSU is going to be going through the dumpsters. Maybe the killer tossed it."

He glanced at the soul. Her gaze didn't waver. He could feel her longing, her desire to speak. Her lips didn't move. He'd seen all types of murders, but rarely did the soul of the victim hang around. The girl couldn't have been more than eighteen or nineteen. So young to have her life ripped away in such a brutal manner.

"Dr. Morana, someone's here for you." A woman's voice broke his concentration.

Patrick looked up in surprise. He saw a female officer holding up the crime scene tape. He was thunderstruck for a moment as a slender young woman ducked under the tape and walked towards him. Her hair was red and pulled back from her face. She had a striking beauty, with large brown eyes that fit well in her face. Her clothes accentuated her petite figure while still appearing collected and professional. She wore a blue oxford shirt and black trousers. She also wore a leather jacket, which was an unusual choice. She was younger than him by maybe six or so years, and she wore an ID tag around her neck.

"Who are you?" Beck asked in the wake of Patrick's silence.

"I'm Dr. Nataliya Vasilyeva," she said smoothly. "I got a call from one of the employees at the morgue, saying to meet Dr. Morana at the crime scene. I guess you're throwing me into the deep end for my first day." She looked between the two men without taking in the body, then turned back to Patrick again, correctly guessing which one he was. "You look surprised to see me."

Patrick stood up. "Um, yes."

"I'm the fellow from Barnes-Jewish." Dr. Vasilyeva licked her lips when the name of the hospital didn't spark recognition. "The Forensic Pathology Fellowship?"

"Oh!" Patrick felt a rush of relief as he remembered. "I'm sorry. Of course. I'm a bit distracted, as you can see. I completely forgot you were starting today. I'd shake your hand, but—" he looked down at his gloves. How old was she to have finished her residency already?

"No worries," she said. "I'm sorry to be a surprise."

Patrick smiled. "It's fine. We can discuss the minutiae later." He turned back to the body and noticed Beck was looking at him. When he met his gaze, Beck rolled his eyes. He was one to judge. Patrick wasn't usually distracted by good looks, but Beck couldn't make the same claim.

"The officers told me it was a teenage girl," Dr. Vasilyeva said, stepping forward. "Any visible marks?"

"None that we can see. We're going to have to do a full autopsy. Have you done one solo yet?"

She shook her head. "No. But I assisted in several in medical school and during my residency."

That was to be expected. "Good." He looked down at the body. There were many reasons she could be dead, but the presence of her soul unnerved him. There was something unnatural about her death. More unnatural than murder, he supposed. "Come on, Dr. Vasilyeva. It looks like the CSU is here." He waved at the crime scene unit who had rolled up. Several onlookers crowded around the area, curious as to what had interrupted their Monday morning.

"When can I expect the COD?" Beck asked. Patrick thought for a moment, going through his day's tasks. Murder cases took priority, and the Cause of Death was important to the investigation.

"This afternoon, I hope. Once CSU is done here, I'll make sure they get samples when I open her up." He escorted Dr. Vasilyeva away from the dead body. "Have you ever been to a crime scene before?" he asked her.

"A couple times last year, but I just observed."

"Very good." Patrick peeled off his gloves and held out his hand. "It's a pleasure to meet you, Dr. Vasilyeva."

She shook it. "Nice to meet you too. You can call me Nataliya if you want. Vasilyeva is already a mouthful, though you do say it perfectly."

A smile twitched on his lips. How many people had fumbled her name? "I'm sorry I didn't recognize you. I've been on sabbatical and wasn't able to conduct the interviews."

"It's fine," Nataliya replied.

"I feel bad that you came down here when I was pretty much done. There wasn't much I could do except confirm her death and put in the autopsy order."

"It's fine," Nataliya repeated. "All part of the job, right?"

"Yes." Something about her put him off-kilter. He shouldn't have been surprised at her attitude. She had to be able to roll with changes if she worked as a doctor. He couldn't remember exactly what she did for most of her residency, as he'd only given her résumé a cursory glance before he went on sabbatical. "I'm going to head back to the morgue," he said. "Do you know where it is?"

"Yes," she said. "I'll meet you there. Do you want me to grab you a coffee or anything?"

Patrick gazed at her, unsure of what she meant by her offer. Sometimes when the new medical examiners came through, they wanted to curry favor by doing little things for him. It was mostly harmless, nothing compared to the complicated politics between the police department, hospital networks, and coroner's office. He had only just met Nataliya, and she seemed remarkably composed considering they'd met over a dead body.

"No, thank you," he said finally. She smiled and walked off, pushing through the crowd of onlookers. Patrick turned to where the CSU was starting to process the crime scene. Beck was talking, giving orders, writing things down. The soul stared at him, silent. It hadn't left yet. Usually, if one stuck around this long, it'd be gone before he left the crime scene. Something was holding this soul back. He hoped it'd be gone before he performed the autopsy. He didn't want the poor soul to be watching as he cracked open the body's rib cage.

Patrick turned away and went to his car. He mentally sifted through what he had to do once the girl's body was delivered to the morgue. Nataliya would expect to either assist or perform the autopsy herself. He didn't work much with new students, at least not since he'd been appointed coroner the year before. His own fellowship had been fraught with politics and difficulties, and he didn't want his new fellow to deal with that.

Unsurprisingly, Patrick beat Nataliya to the morgue. He went straight to his office and dug around in his file cabinet to find her résumé and the notes the county board had taken when they selected her for the fellowship. His long-time friend and city coroner Travis McCormick had done most of the interviewing for him.

Nataliya Vasilyeva was twenty-six, and it appeared she'd graduated with her BS in biology when she was only nineteen. She had amazing references with an absolutely flawless record. She worked in pathology at Barnes-Jewish Hospital, which meant her letters of recommendation were impressive. It looked as if McCormick had wanted to poach her, based on his effusive praise for the young woman. *Genius*, he'd written. *I'm surprised she wants to work as a medical examiner; she has the talent, skills, and deductive mind of a top-notch emergency surgeon or diagnostician. She's well-spoken, driven, and exactly what you need in your morgue, Patrick. You'd be an idiot to pass her up. No other candidate will come close to her level of skill. I watched her videos from her classes and residency surgeries, and I can tell you she has one of the most iron stomachs I've ever seen in a doctor of her age.*

Patrick drummed his fingers on the desktop. He glanced at her résumé again. She was fluent in Russian, which was hardly a surprise. Her education was impressive as well, Northwestern for undergrad, and then WashU medical school. She'd been in St. Louis for several years, then. He wished he could have been there for the interviews. He would have liked to get a good sense of her before they started working together. McCormick was reliable, and Patrick was sure he'd get along fine with Nataliya. But going in blind didn't really suit him.

He heard a knock on the door. One of the other examiners poked his head in. "You're back," he said. "Did you meet Dr. Vasilyeva yet?"

Patrick looked up at Dr. Hammond. He was older, had no interest in career advancement, and was content doing the humdrum, noncriminal autopsies. No surprises. No testifying in court cases. Reliable work hours and a paycheck. "Yes," Patrick replied, hoping that Nataliya had a bit more ambition than that. Though judging by her résumé, references, and the notes, she did.

"How is she?"

"She seems competent," Patrick replied. "The transporters should be bringing the body in an hour or so after processing."

"We just got a body from SLU," Hammond said. "Older fella, not sure why he went down."

"All right. Work on him and send your report over. With Dr. Vasilyeva here, you can have an early one."

Hammond grinned. "Thanks, kid," he said, and disappeared. Hammond was nearing retirement, which meant his hours were more part-time. That suited Patrick fine, especially with a new fellow coming in to do more work. "Fresh meat is here!" Hammond's voice rang through the hallway.

Patrick sighed and got up from his desk. He left his office and went to the front desk. The receptionist was chatting with Nataliya, who had a coffee cup in her hand. "We have a break room," Denise said, "if you ever want to bring anything in for your breaks. We have some strict rules about what can go where, but I can go over them later. Oh, hello, Dr. Morana." Denise, who was even older than Dr. Hammond, grinned at him behind her cat's eye glasses. He couldn't ever imagine the lady retiring, and it would be a sad day when she left.

Nataliya turned and smiled at him. "Hello again!" she said.

"Hello," he replied, returning the smile. It felt more natural than it would have over a dead body. "Welcome to the morgue. Come on, I'll show you around."

"Aren't you busy?" Nataliya asked, glancing at Denise for a quick second.

"Yes, but you'll be working very closely with me, and I didn't get a chance to interview you." He beckoned for her to walk around the front desk. "Good morning, Denise," he said. "How's Howard?"

"Wonderful. Good to see you back, finally." Denise tapped her pen against the earpiece of her glasses. "I was beginning to think you were going to stay in New York forever."

"God forbid," Patrick said. He'd gone to New York City to aid in a medical research project during his sabbatical, and it hadn't been the relaxing time off he'd hoped for. Coming back to his morgue had been a relief.

Partick led Nataliya into the back hallway. "Three examiners, including myself, work here on a regular basis. Dr. Hammond only works part time. His office is there. He shares with Dr. Paulson. She splits her time between here and teaching at SLU. We have other medical examiners come in on a case-by-case basis and if we're busy. This is my office." He opened the door. "We don't have another room for an office, so you can share with me."

"Really?" Nataliya asked.

"I figured it'd be best, since I am here to supervise you. We can bring in another desk." He gestured for her to sit on one of the extra chairs across from his desk. He sat down behind it. Nataliya removed her leather jacket and hung it on a hook by the door, then she sat down and crossed her legs. She sipped at her coffee, waiting for him to speak again.

"I've never had a fellow before," Patrick said.

"That's what Dr. McCormick said in our first interview. Dr. Morana, I have to ask, do you want me here? I got the feeling from Dr. McCormick that you're not exactly a people person."

Patrick was taken aback at her blunt question. "What?"

"He just seemed concerned that it might be hard to transition from working at a big hospital to coming here and working under you."

"That's a natural concern for anyone choosing to be a medical examiner," Patrick said. "I think you'll do fine. I don't know why Dr. McCormick would give you that impression. We've known each other for a long time, since my residency."

"Good. I just want to be upfront with any concerns," she said. "My best friend says I'm too blunt for my own good when I'm curious about something. It's the Russian in me, I think." She gave him a lopsided smile.

"Blunt can be good, especially in this line of work. With other doctors, that is, maybe not with families." Patrick chuckled.

"Good." She took a long drink of coffee. "You're younger than I thought you'd be."

"You didn't google me?" he asked with a smirk. "I could say the same for you."

"You didn't read my résumé?" she asked back, matching his smirk.

"Full concession, I barely glanced at it before I left on sabbatical. I fully trust Dr. McCormick's judgment, and I believe you'll do very well." His phone buzzed, and he saw that Denise was texting him to let him know the body of the teenage girl had arrived. He put the phone down on his desk and stood up. Nataliya stood too. "All right, Dr. Nataliya Vasilyeva. Finish your coffee. Your fellowship starts right now."

CHAPTER TWO

Instead of entering the autopsy suite right away, Nataliya waited, peering inside through the steel-framed glass window. At Patrick's suggestion, she'd finished her coffee and grabbed one of the long gowns to wear over her clothing. Her hair was already tied back, but she twisted it up under a surgical cap. She watched Dr. Morana as he readied the room for the autopsy. She'd never answered his question; she had googled him before applying for the fellowship. But she didn't find much beyond his education, not even a photograph. That seemed odd, considering he must have been involved in court cases as a coroner. Regardless, her surprise at his age was genuine. While he wasn't as devastatingly handsome as Detective Beck (in spite of his obvious hangover), he had an understated handsomeness to him. He carried himself with a weight of responsibility, and as he laid out the tools of their trade, he moved with marked efficiency. He had no wasted movements, no lingering side thoughts as he set up the video camera. His dark hair was hidden beneath his own surgical cap, and he hadn't yet put gloves over his slender hands. That was perhaps most curious to her. She always looked at people's hands. Most of her friends did, coming through medical school as they did. They observed so many surgeries that it was second nature to take note of the shape and deftness of one's fingers.

Dr. Morana's hands were beautiful, with well-trimmed nails and not a scar in sight. This far away, she couldn't see much, but in his office, she'd glanced more than once at the shape of his fingers. What did Alex call them? Pianist fingers? She wondered if Patrick played the piano. It would fit with the image she was building of him. He was probably only about 32 years old or so, though he had the gravitas of the older doctors she worked with. This man chose a field that involved unending daily contact with the dead. And yet. . .

And yet he seemed to lack the good humor of Dr. McCormick or the seriousness of some of her instructors. He was polite and utterly unreadable. She rolled her eyes at herself and entered through the swinging doors.

"Are you ready?" Dr. Morana asked. "I'm going to take the lead on this one."

She didn't argue. While going to the crime scene on her first day was a surprise, she was expecting him to take the lead on autopsies, at least for a bit. Dr. Morana started recording and took measurements of the body, noting out loud the weight, size, and physical description of the body and clothing. Without being asked, Nataliya wrote everything down on the clipboard by the autopsy table. After removing the victim's clothes and bagging them for processing, Dr. Morana continued examination of her body. She didn't have any abnormal bruising, just faded bruises on her legs from random encounters with a chair or bed frame that the Jane Doe probably hadn't even noticed. Nataliya made a note of each bruise on the diagrams, and she also noted that both ears had several piercings, with the jewelry gone. Jane Doe had no tattoos or birthmarks. Her pristine appearance was marred when they got to the rape examination. "Indication of forced penetration by a foreign object. I'm not sure what, but perhaps it was a sexual organ, or something similar."

Nataliya frowned and wrote it down.

"Put the block under her, please," Dr. Morana said once the external exam was finished. She put down the clipboard and grabbed the rubber block. Dr. Morana lifted the torso, and Nataliya placed the block under her shoulders. With a glance at the head of the body, he hesitated for a moment. The hesitation seemed at odds with the rest of his exam, but he turned back and took hold of his scalpel. He made the Y incision with practiced ease. Nataliya wondered if she'd get that good at it by the time she was his age. He took a deep breath and pulled the skin back. He shook his head, as if shaking off some lingering thought, and continued on with his work without any of his prior hesitation. He cut the rib cage, the snap and crunch of the rib cutter edging out their silence. He set the sternum piece aside and began his internal examination. "At first glance, the organs seem normal," he said. He inspected them one by one, nothing out of the ordinary for a girl in her late teens.

Until he got to her heart. He frowned as he pulled it from the chest cavity. "This is very strange," he said.

Nataliya moved closer so that she could see as he turned it around in the light. "What the hell?" The heart was misshapen, as if someone had squeezed the muscle like a hunk of Play-Doh.

Dr. Morana moved the organ one way and then the other, looking at it from all angles. "I have never seen or heard of this, ever." He put it on the scale. "The weight is normal. I have no idea how she could have lived with a heart that looks like this."

"Could that have been what killed her?" Nataliya asked.

Patrick didn't reply for a moment as he looked at the misshapen heart. "Most likely. I don't know how this could have occurred, though. We didn't see any signs of trauma to her chest. How could her heart collapse like that?" He sighed and put the heart into formalin to preserve it until later. "Everything else so far has been normal." He had taken the contents of her stomach to be analyzed, along with urine, blood, and other tissues. Nataliya didn't know what to think about the heart. If the body had been mangled, she might have been able to understand the misshapen organ. But the girl looked normal. Dead, but normal.

They continued on with the autopsy, the heart at the back of her mind. They removed the block from underneath her torso and began the brain extraction. Like everything else, the brain was normal. "So I guess it was the heart," Nataliya said as Dr. Morana finished his examination of the brain.

"It looks to be that way. We'll know more when we get the toxicology screens, but a crushed heart would certainly do the trick. That's not going to go over well with Beck."

"The detective?" she asked.

"Yes. He's got his work cut out for him. A rape victim in the Central West End is definitely cause for concern. Not to mention the fact that we can't conclude she was murdered."

Nataliya finished writing all her notes and helped him to reconstitute the body. She'd done her share of that work in medical school and the autopsies she assisted with during her residency.

It was a puzzle in and of itself, trying to figure out why someone died, then putting them back together again. They still didn't know who the girl was. It would take a while before DNA and fingerprint comparisons would yield any results, if she was even in a system anywhere. She supposed Detective Beck and the rest of the officers were scouring missing persons reports and putting the word out that they'd found a Jane Doe with her description. Who knew how long it would be until they could get any sort of identification?

"All right, Dr. Vasilyeva, stitch her up." Dr. Morana stepped back and stripped off his gloves. She stepped into his place without further urging. He seemed to switch between calling her by her first name and Dr. Vasilyeva. She didn't think about that, she had to concentrate. It wasn't as sensitive as if she were stitching up a live patient, but she had standards and she wanted to impress Dr. Morana. She stitched the Y incision until it looked as if they'd never pulled out the dead girl's insides and poked and prodded and dissected them. Though she had a good poker face, she was always a bit in awe of what happened during surgeries and autopsies. It was more than a puzzle sometimes, to take organs out and replace them and have the body in better working order. Everything was connected, and she still marveled at the power she held in her hands.

"Good," Dr. Morana said when she finished the last stitch. He turned off the video camera. She helped him move the body into the cooler until the girl could be identified.

"Finish up your notes and then you can take a break. Good work." Dr. Morana smiled at her now that the dead body was out of sight, and then he left the room. Nataliya let out a deep breath. It felt like she'd been holding it in for the entire autopsy. It wasn't until that moment that she realized how much the man intimidated her. She didn't know why, he was certainly kind enough and praised her. But he was so adept at his job, and with Dr. McCormick's warnings that Patrick Morana was something of an odd duck, she didn't know what to expect.

It was no use fretting about. She needed to make sure her notes were crystal clear. Even if the dead girl wasn't murdered, she was raped. If they found out who did it to her, they'd need comprehensive notes. She let out another deep breath and went back to work.

CHAPTER THREE

Nataliya rubbed her temples as she waited for her coffee to brew. She was glad that the morgue had a coffee maker in the kitchenette. Her phone rang, startling her out of her sleepy reverie. It was too early for phone calls, and she frowned when she saw the name on the screen.

She picked up the phone and sighed before answering. "Dr. Vasilyeva."

"You know who it is, Talya." The man's voice was tired, but smooth as velvet.

She licked her lips. "Alex, I don't want to talk to you. I'm about to clock in."

"What are you doing there so early?"

"Working," she said, her voice curt. "What are you doing calling me?"

"I had some time before my surgeries today." Alex let out his own sigh. Just hearing his voice made Nataliya want to close her eyes and daydream. She missed him, but she wasn't in love with him anymore. "Look, I just want to talk to you. We ended on such a sour note. I don't want to let this dangle over me."

"What else is there to say, Alex? Besides, I'm not going to discuss this with you over the phone when I'm only five days into this new job."

"I know, I know. I just wanted to meet up after work today. I got invited to a couple of Halloween parties, but I know that's not your thing."

Nataliya heard the coffee maker sputter, the last drops falling into the glass urn. She stood up and went to serve herself a cup. She had a lot of organizing to do with her notes before her first autopsy of the day. Alex was distracting her already. "I'm going out tonight to get drinks with some people," she said.

"Who?"

"Why do you care?"

Alex groaned. "I'm just curious. God, Nataliya. I just want to talk to you about this. I talked to Eva, and she said—"

"Look, I left for a reason, and I was upfront with you about that. Can't you let it go?"

Dr. Morana walked into the room then, Denise at his heels. Nataliya managed a fake smile as he helped himself to coffee. She noted he liked it black, and Denise liked hers with way too much sugar to be healthy.

"I can't, Talya. I love you. I never wanted things to end. I want you back," Alex said, the pleading in his voice real.

"Well, I don't want you back. I can't talk now." Nataliya tried to lower her voice.

"Why not? Is your boss there?"

"Yes."

Both Denise and Dr. Morana pretended not to hear her conversation, for which she was grateful. The last thing she needed was for her coworkers to think her relationship drama would interfere with her work.

"I gotta go," Nataliya added. "I'll text you later." She hung up before he could say goodbye and put her phone into her pocket. "Good morning," she said.

"Good morning, Talya," Denise said. Nataliya had given her permission to use her nickname on the second day of work. She didn't say so to Dr. Morana, still feeling distant from him. He called her Dr. Visilyeva when they were being professional, and Nataliya when they were just chatting. It was strange to her, but she appreciated it. He respected her as a doctor.

Without greeting her, Dr. Morana went right into business. "Dr. Vasilyeva, we might have found the identity of the Jane Doe. A woman, I think the mother, is coming to ID the body soon. I want you to be there."

"Of course, Dr. Morana," Nataliya replied. She hadn't experienced an ID before, and she definitely didn't want to misstep. It was a delicate thing, and she had heard stories where families had denied their loved ones were dead, even with DNA proof.

Dr. Morana nodded in approval and left the room to do his paperwork in their shared office.

After finishing her coffee and chatting with Denise about her grandkids' Halloween costumes, Nataliya rinsed out her coffee mug and followed Dr. Morana. It felt a bit odd, having someone come in to identify a body on Halloween.

Dr. Morana was elbow deep in his file cabinets, literally. "Nataliya, I forgot to mention that Agent Lyons is coming tonight."

"Who?"

He looked up from the drawer. "The FBI agent that Jason Beck has been working with."

"I only talked to him twice," Nataliya said with a smile. "I don't remember much about an FBI agent. Just what we told him about the autopsy."

"Oh, of course. Well, she's only been in St. Louis for a couple of months. I don't know her well either, which I guess is why Beck invited her."

Nataliya sat down at her desk and started filling out her own paperwork. The one aspect of the job she was not fond of. Her thoughts drifted a bit. Alex really hadn't been the jealous type while they were dating, but she wasn't about to tell him she was getting drinks with her boss and a homicide detective who was also a man. She let him assume it was with her friends from her residency at Barnes. Eva, her roommate, was working all night. She was an ER nurse, and she was rather salty that she couldn't go to the big Halloween party in Dogtown. Nataliya regretted taking Eva up on the offer of renting an apartment together, but she couldn't move out until next summer since her name was on the lease.

"I hope I'm not expected to wear a costume tonight," Nataliya said over the rustling of file folders.

Dr. Morana let out a cackling laugh. It was so unlike him that she looked up in surprise. He was grinning. "Sorry, sorry," he said, shaking his head. "I hate Halloween."

She could have figured that out; he was so staid. "Okay, good. It's not my favorite either."

"Beck is too depressed to care one way or the other, and Agent Lyons doesn't seem like the type to wear a costume out on the town."

Nataliya was about to reply when Denise poked her head into the open door. "Dr. Morana, Mr. and Mrs. Ingle are here."

"Thank you, Denise." Dr. Morana put the rest of the file folders back in the cabinet.

Nataliya took a deep breath and stood up. She didn't know what to expect. She followed Dr. Morana out of their office and into the exam room. Nataliya had stayed late the day before, cleaning it. She was grateful now that she'd decided to do the deep clean a day early.

"Are you nervous?" Dr. Morana asked her when she cracked her knuckles.

"I have never done this before," she admitted.

"You don't have to say anything." Dr. Morana smiled at her, and she managed a feeble smile back. "Just observe."

Denise led a middle-aged couple into the exam room. Detective Beck came in with them. Nataliya had forgotten that he would need to be present for the ID for his case file. She didn't acknowledge him as he stood next to Dr. Morana. Nataliya took a few steps back until she was closer to the autopsy table.

"I'm sorry to meet under these circumstances," Dr. Morana said.

"Please, can we just get this over with?" Mr. Ingle asked.

"Of course. My apologies." Dr. Morana unlocked the cooler door and pulled out the body of the Jane Doe. With his efficient movements, he folded down the sheet just above the Y incision to show the corpse's face.

Mrs. Ingle let out a cry of disbelief and slapped her hand over her mouth to muffle the ensuing sobs. Her husband quickly pulled her into his arms and tucked her head into his shoulder. "That's Jamie," he said, his voice wavering. "That's my little baby."

"I'm very sorry for your loss," Dr. Morana said. He shared a glance with Beck, who was taking notes.

"How did she die?" Mr. Ingle asked.

Dr. Morana licked his lips. This time he looked over at Nataliya. Beck had been just as flummoxed as they had been when he was told the cause of death.

"It appears her heart collapsed," he said.

"What?" Mr. Ingle's voice was a croak. "What do you mean? Was it a defect?"

"I don't know, unfortunately. I've never seen anything like it. From what I could discern, the heart seemed to collapse, which of course made it stop beating. That was the cause of death."

"There's something else, Mr. and Mrs. Ingle," Beck said. He scratched behind his ear. "She had signs of sexual assault."

"She was raped?" Mrs. Ingle asked, whipping her head around. "Why didn't she tell us?"

"Mrs. Ingle, the sexual assault happened very close to the time that she died. I highly doubt she had time to tell anyone," Dr. Morana explained.

"Do you think someone murdered her?" Mrs. Ingle's voice rose in pitch.

"I don't see how that would be possible, ma'am." Dr. Morana shrugged. "But we are still waiting on her blood tests and tox screens. There's always a chance she ingested something or was forced to ingest something."

"We're doing everything we can," Beck continued. "We're going to look at this from every angle, I promise you."

Unsurprisingly, the Ingles didn't look comforted.

"We'll arrange for her body to be sent to the funeral home," Dr. Morana said gently.

"Her—her body?!" Mr. Ingle shouted. "She's not just a body."

"I understand. I'm sorry." Dr. Morana took the man's anger in stride. His calm expression didn't crack. Nataliya fought the urge to gape at the angry father.

"I told her to stay home," Mr. Ingle said, tears streaming down his cheeks. "I didn't want her to stay on campus. Oh god. Oh, Jamie." He reached for Jamie's face but he stopped short of touching her. "Cover her back up."

Dr. Morana did so. He pushed the body back into the cooler and locked the door. Mrs. Ingle was weeping now. She clung to her husband.

Nataliya bit her lip as the sad group left the exam room to speak with Denise about arrangements. Beck would also have more questions for them. Jamie. It was odd to have a name for the Jane Doe. It made the whole business seem sadder. Like having a name made the dead body real. Nataliya licked her lips, trying clear her thoughts. How foolish. She'd assisted on autopsies with named people.

She went back to the office, pondering what had happened. She wondered if she could ever be as calm and soothing as Dr. Morana. It was as if he knew just how to act to make himself unobtrusive. His voice had been gentle, deep and soft. A comforting voice. Not that it would help to a pair of grieving parents. But he was exactly who she'd want to tell her a loved one was dead.

It wasn't until Dr. Morana returned to the office that she realized she had gotten lost in thought.

"Victims of violence are always the hardest," he said. He sat down at his desk. "When they have to be identified like that. And kids." He shook his head. "It doesn't get any easier. I don't want you to think for a minute that this job gets easier. You get better at it, of course, but that part? It's the hardest. I'd rather testify in court every day than show a dead child to her mother."

Nataliya took in his words. Dr. Morana was so self-assured otherwise. His honesty touched her. Alex was so different from him. He had a bravado about him, not quite arrogance but something else. Alex would never have admitted to someone he was supervising that he still had trouble with some aspect of being a neurosurgeon. Oh, he'd shared his fears with her more than once. But to someone he was supposed to mentor? Certainly not. She didn't begrudge Alex his attitude. He needed it to play the hospital politics and to be the best surgeon in his department.

"Are you all right?" Dr. Morana asked when she didn't reply.

"Yes. I'm fine." She didn't smile. She looked up at Dr. Morana. His green eyes held hers. "It just makes you think. About what you'll leave behind when you go."

"Do you think about that a lot?"

"No. I move forward, I guess. I don't want to live a life of regrets. But I also don't want to be too concerned about every single little thing in my life and forget what's important. I never thought this job would be easy. Death isn't easy."

Something akin to a smile tugged at Dr. Morana's lips. "No. It sure isn't," he said, though she wasn't sure what about that statement was funny.

"I only hope that someday I can be as calm and collected as you are when I have family come in to identify bodies. And don't think I'm sucking up. I hate sucking up."

"I believe you." His good humor increased, but he still didn't give a full-out smile. "Finish your paperwork. You have an autopsy to perform after lunch."

CHAPTER FOUR

McRand's was a nice pub not too far from the morgue. Patrick liked it because it attracted a different crowd than near University City or Dogtown. Another thing he liked about it was they never celebrated any holiday except St. Patrick's Day and Christmas. There was no one in costume in the little pub save a young woman wearing cat ears. Even that looked half-hearted.

Patrick settled down in his usual booth. He'd changed clothes at the morgue, eschewing his professional suit for jeans and a hoodie. Not a moment later Beck walked in, similarly attired. Without prompting, one of the McRand ladies brought out a Tullamore Dew for Patrick and Paddy for Beck. They'd been drinking the same whiskeys on Halloween ever since they met.

"Evening," Patrick said after they received their drinks. "How did questioning the Ingles go?"

"Not great," Beck replied. He knocked back his whiskey. "I can't tell you too much, but they haven't had much contact with their daughter since she left for college. I'm going to interview her roommate on Monday. I just don't know what we can do with this case. We have no evidence to even begin to find who did it. We don't even know if she was murdered."

Patrick sipped at his whiskey. He wondered how much he should tell Beck about the autopsy. He hadn't been prepared for how difficult it would be with the soul of the dead girl watching him. Every time he passed the exam room while her body lay in the cooler, the soul would stare at him, her yearning to speak ever more pressing. She finally left when her body was sent to the funeral home. He had never seen a soul stick around so long. She had been murdered, but he had no idea how to relate this to Beck. Patrick couldn't straight up tell the detective that magic had crushed her heart.

The door of the pub opened with a blast of late October chill. Nataliya hurried in, wearing the same clothes she had at work. Her hair was down, though, falling over her shoulders like a red waterfall. Spying the two of them, she came over and sat down next to Patrick. "Hey there, Detective Beck," she said with a bright smile.

"Just Beck. I'm only 'Detective' on the clock." He saluted her with his empty glass. Rhonda, the woman who served them earlier, came over as soon as she saw Nataliya. She put another glass of Paddy in front of Beck.

"What'll you have, honey?" she asked, meeting Nataliya's eyes.

"Vodka tonic," she said.

Rhonda chuckled. "Quite a bit different from these gentlemen."

"I tell myself it's because I'm Russian, but frankly I think that's just an excuse," Nataliya replied. "I got used to drinking it in medical school because that's what my roommate always bought."

Patrick wondered if it was because her roommate would have been old enough to buy liquor, while Nataliya was nineteen when she first attended.

"Be right back with that." Rhonda smiled and turned back to the bar.

Nataliya shed her coat and ran her fingers through her hair. "I am so ready to unwind," she said.

"Me too," Beck sighed, downing the Paddy as quickly as he had the first. "Elise is trying to get the house."

Nataliya glanced at Patrick who shook his head. She didn't say anything.

"Sorry, man," Patrick said.

"Gonna forget about her tonight," Beck said with a vigor that Patrick knew was fake. He'd be four whiskeys in and try to call her, wherein Patrick would confiscate his phone until it was time to call for a ride.

Rhonda returned with another whiskey for Beck and Nataliya's vodka tonic. "Here you go, honey."

"Thank you," Nataliya said, flashing another smile. She turned back to the two men. "I'm really enjoying this job, Dr. Morana. I don't miss the frantic pace of working the ER or even the hospital in general. It's still quite a culture shock, I guess. The patients don't talk to you."

"Yeah, if they did, it'd make my job a whole lot easier," Beck muttered. "Patrick here has helped me solve more than a few cases since he was appointed coroner. He's a lot easier to work with than the last coroner y'all had in there. Dr. Goodwin was a lot more comfortable with the dead than any of the living. Gave me the creeps."

"I hate to hear that," Patrick said. "Just because we work with the dead doesn't mean we don't need good people skills."

Nataliya sipped at her drink. "As I've discovered today. Watching the Ingles was difficult."

"Patrick here is a pro," Beck said, leaning back in the booth. Before he got too comfortable, he leaned forward again with a lazy smile. "Julie is here."

"Julie?" Nataliya asked.

Beck waved toward the door while Patrick answered her.

"Special Agent Julie Lyons," Patrick explained.

"Oh, right, I forgot she was coming. I haven't met her yet." Nataliya fiddled with the straw in her glass.

A tall woman with raven hair strode towards the table. She walked with purpose, daring anyone to get in her way. She wasn't dressed as she usually did for work, choosing instead to wear Doc Martens, black skinny jeans, and a tight gray tank top under a motorcycle jacket.

"Happy Halloween," she said, sliding into the booth next to Beck. "You must be Dr. Vasilyeva." She stumbled a bit over the name, but quickly corrected herself.

"Please, Nataliya. And it's a bit shorter to say."

Julie reached over the table to shake hands. "Julie Lyons. I see you're well into your cups, Beck."

Beck just grunted. As if on cue, Rhonda came to the table. "Whatcha havin', Julie?" she asked.

Julie tapped her chin. "I'm feeling crappy tonight. Surprise me. Also bring out a plate of nachos for the table."

"Coming right up." Rhonda twirled away.

"What has you down?" Beck asked.

Julie frowned and turned to look at him. "I just got a case in Alton that has everyone completely baffled. Some girl was found on the riverfront, dead, no visible marks. She was sexually assaulted. The coroner's report said her heart had collapsed."

"Are you fucking kidding me?" Beck asked, dropping his glass on the table with unexpected force.

"Yeah, insane, right?" Julie shook her head.

"No, I mean—" He let out a growl of frustration. "Alton is across state lines. I guess we'll be working together again."

"What are you talking about?" Julie asked.

"I just did an autopsy on Monday with the exact same cause of death," Patrick replied before Beck could. "Like something had squeezed the girl's heart until it was completely misshapen."

"Oh shit," Julie said. "The Alton case was about a month ago, but it took this long to process her blood tests. She didn't have anything in her system other than a bit of marijuana. She'd eaten some herbs before she died. Which is weird, because there wasn't anything else in her stomach. Who eats whole leaves with nothing else?" She threw up her hands. "Two girls died in the same manner, a month apart. What are the odds of two girls with hearts like this?"

"I've never seen this, ever," Patrick said. He glanced at Nataliya.

"You've seen more than me," she said. "I've certainly never heard of it."

"I'd better call the metropolitan area stations," Julie said with a heavy sigh. "We need to see if there are any similar cases. Though with how unusual they are, I'm sure we would have heard about it before now."

"Scoot," Beck said, pushing Julie on the arm. "Gonna call the station and get whoever's on desk duty to mark Jamie Ingle's roommate for an interview as soon as possible. Julie, we're going to need to talk and try to connect the dots." Julie glared at him but got out of the booth. Both of them left the pub, their phones in hand.

Nataliya let out a breath. "What do you think this means?" she asked, turning to face Patrick.

"I don't know," Patrick replied. Of course, he did know. But she would think he was crazy if he told her. He had to think. How could he nudge Beck and the FBI in the right direction? The fact that the case was so unusual meant their suspicions were up, in spite of the impossibility of murder. Whoever was raping these girls, murdering them, was not going to stop. He knew enough about sexual-based crimes to know that.

"Are they going to go back to work?" she asked.

"I doubt Beck will. He's had too much to drink already. I don't know about Julie. I don't know her very well."

Nataliya let out a sigh. "I certainly didn't bargain for this when I applied for the fellowship."

"One thing you'll learn pretty fast is that you will see far more unusual deaths than you thought you would, in between the heart attacks and car accidents and overdoses." Patrick sipped at his whiskey. Nataliya was skilled, she'd proven that. She wasn't bothered by dead bodies. It was the emotion of the families that would be hard for her. But he knew she was going to do well, even after a week—anyone in his line of work would be able to see that.

"Talya!"

The voice startled Nataliya so badly that she jumped in her seat. "*Blyat*, what's he doing here?"

A very handsome man rushed over to the booth. He had curling blond hair and was wearing scrubs. "I was hoping to catch you," he said, not even glancing at Patrick.

"What are you doing here, Alex?" Nataliya said, jumping to her feet. "How'd you even know where I was?"

"Eva told me. I know you, Talya, you were going to ghost me." He looked over her shoulder and saw Patrick for the first time. He straightened up, his eyes wide with surprise.

"This is my boss, Dr. Patrick Morana," Nataliya said, stepping aside to present Patrick. He felt very awkward as he shook hands with the other man. "Dr. Morana, this is my ex-boyfriend Dr. Alexander Wingate."

"Nice to meet you," Alex said in a rush. He turned to her. "I'm sorry for the stalker behavior. I promise I'll never do it again. You know this isn't me."

Nataliya didn't say anything. She crossed her arms.

Alex looked at Patrick again and took her arm. "Come on, let's talk over here."

Patrick watched with a bit of puzzlement as the two walked over to the bar. It was still too early in the evening for live music, and the piped-in music was too soft to cover their conversation.

He sipped at his whiskey, eavesdropping on their conversation. He wasn't normally the sort to do such a thing, but he could hardly help it. He had excellent hearing, and Nataliya was not keeping her voice down in her anger.

"I'm sorry to do it this way, but I really needed to see you," Alex said.

"Why?" Nataliya didn't bother to soften her tone.

"You never even gave me a chance, Talya. You blindsided me with your decision. One day we're going along, happily in love, and the next day, you tell me you're leaving me."

"If you think we were happily in love, you weren't paying attention. You told me I was wasting my life."

Alex stiffened, and Patrick fought the urge to stare in surprise.

"That's not what I said, Nataliya."

"Oh? Maybe not in those exact words, but how else was I supposed to take it? You said that someone with my talent should be helping people."

Alex didn't reply. Patrick felt a growing sense of unease that had nothing to do with watching two exes fight. Was that what people thought about him? If a boyfriend said that to his girlfriend, what would strangers think about him? He didn't much care what people thought about him personally, but he didn't want anyone to smear the profession. And Nataliya didn't deserve that attitude at all.

"I didn't mean—I don't think you're wasting your life as a medical examiner. But I think you also passed up some amazing opportunities. You could have done anything, Nataliya. You have such a knack for figuring out what's wrong with someone, even when they can't put their hurt into words. I just feel like you never properly explored all of your options."

Nataliya rubbed her eyes. "Alex. I told you that I wanted to be a medical examiner to help people. And you deliberately refused to understand what I meant. You didn't even ask. You were too focused on your own career and your own problems to do anything more than pass quick judgment on me. I didn't dump you just because of what you said. I dumped you because our relationship was all about you. You didn't make enough of an effort. I loved you so much, but that faded when I realized that the most important thing to you is your career. I didn't want this wall to be built between us, for us to get married and have kids. I didn't want to do that only to get twenty years down the line and realize I married you only because you wanted me to. You're an amazing doctor, Alex, and I admire you so much. I care about you still, as much as I wish I didn't. But I can't be who you want me to be. I can't go work at Barnes with you and be the Power Couple who ends up running the hospital someday. I don't want that."

"What do you want, then? I'm asking now."

Nataliya glanced over at Patrick and met his eyes for a brief moment. She turned back to Alex. "I told you, I want to help people. I want to be with someone who asks me that question, long before we get to this point. I wanted to be a medical examiner because of what you said. I do know how to figure out what's wrong with someone when they can't put it into words themselves. The dead can't speak, Alex. They can't demand justice, they can't tell us what killed them, a person or a disease or a defect of their heart. Someone has to speak for them. Yes, I could have been any kind of doctor at all. I could have been a plastic surgeon and made more money than I would know what to do with. I could have been a pediatric neurosurgeon and saved the lives of the most vulnerable. I could have used my talents and skills to heal people. But that's not what I want to do. There are plenty of amazing doctors like you, Alex. So please, don't try to guilt me over this."

Patrick had stopped drinking. He didn't bother to hide his stare. Nataliya's words ricocheted around his mind. She wanted to speak for the dead. He thought of the dead girl they'd just identified. The soul who had wanted to speak but could not move her lips. He had to speak for her, but he'd lied. The girl didn't leave during the autopsy because he lied to Nataliya and to Beck and her parents. Now that he was hearing Nataliya vehemently defend her decision to become a medical examiner, he understood. She wanted the truth to be spoken, and it was his responsibility. He looked down at his glass of whiskey, almost gone. Nataliya's words had shamed him, but they also invigorated him. She was young and full of passion. He wanted that passion. It had been so long since he'd been so passionate. He wasn't sure if he had ever felt that way.

"I'm sorry," Alex said after a very long moment. "I'm sorry I never asked. Sometimes it's hard not to get a god complex in this line of work, you know?"

Patrick had met more than a few narcissistic surgeons. Not to mention cops on power trips and politicians who played with legislation like checkers. He didn't know how he felt about Alex yet. The other doctor was in love with Nataliya, which Patrick figured was good taste. It was hard to discern this argument between exes or only a lover's quarrel in an empty Irish pub on Halloween.

"What's up with them?" Rhonda asked, adjusting her apron. She was clearing Beck's empty glasses.

"They used to date," Patrick said.

"Used to? Honey, that's not 'used to.'"

"What?" He turned back in a snap. He felt a strange tightening in his chest as he saw Alex kissing Nataliya. Correction: They were kissing each other. Nataliya certainly wasn't pulling away.

"Where are the others?" Rhonda asked, clearly uninterested in the couple making out at the bar.

"Work," Patrick said. "They're calling their respective superiors. I guess they'll be working together."

"I don't know that FBI girl well, but I've seen how she and Beck snipe at each other," Rhonda said. She still held the empty glasses as she chatted with him. "That's going to be a disaster. You want another drink?"

"No," Patrick said. He downed the last swallow of his whiskey. "Here." He dropped three twenties on the table. "Happy Halloween."

"Patrick!"

"Just keep the change. If Beck and Julie come back in, let them know I paid. I'm gonna head home. Make sure Beck doesn't drive."

Patrick smiled at Rhonda and left the bar, passing by the kissing couple quickly. Somehow he felt like a fifth wheel at this get-together.

Patrick's birthday was on November 1st, though he'd never told anyone. He didn't like celebrating it in the traditional way, but when he and Beck would close down McRand's, he enjoyed being with his best friend. And it seemed like he wouldn't have that this year. It was all right. He'd spent many birthdays alone.

CHAPTER FIVE

Nataliya jerked awake at the sound of an unfamiliar ringtone.

"Wingate."

She fought the urge to groan at the sound of Alex's voice. He continued speaking, still stretched out beside her. In the dark room, she could just barely make out the still ceiling fan. His blackout curtains were one of the things she missed from dating him. "How long ago did his vitals drop? Okay. Dammit. Okay. I don't know, we can't go back in now. Any more trauma would only speed things up."

Nataliya rolled over to watch as Alex sat up on the bed and tried to find his boxers with one foot. "No, I'll come in as soon as I can. I'll have to talk to his parents. Okay. Bye." He hung up the phone and pulled on his boxers. "Sorry, Talya. One of my patients is declining."

"Don't apologize," Nataliya said.

Alex smiled at her and touched her cheek. "You're amazing. I won't stay long. I should be back in about an hour." He kissed her and got out of bed to get dressed. Nataliya peeked at the digital clock on Alex's nightstand. 7:39 AM. Not as early as she thought. Alex left without another word and she sat up. It had been three months since she'd been in Alex's house, and he hadn't changed much. She'd spent so much time over here so they wouldn't bother Eva. The nurse worked the overnight shift and she jealously guarded her nights off. There had even been a time when Nataliya had thought she'd be living in Alex's house, for real, before too long. That was when she was still in denial about how their relationship was just coasting along, without communication and without mutual respect.

Nataliya took a shower, surprised that Alex hadn't thrown out the shampoo she'd bought so long ago. He really did think he'd get her back. When she finished, she went into the kitchen to find something to eat. She supposed Alex hadn't been wrong. All it had taken was him listening to her and a kiss to get her right back in his house. Using his shower. Going through his cupboards for a box of cereal. Sniffing the milk in his fridge. Feeding Popsicle, his Maine Coon. The cat was the largest Nataliya had ever seen, and also the laziest creature in the universe. Half the time the chubby creature would lie on the ground while eating his food.

Nataliya sat on the floor in her clothes from the day before and scratched Popsicle behind the ears as he ate. "I'm such an idiot, Pops." She let out a sigh. "It's going to be even harder to make a clean break. I missed you though."

Popsicle purred, content that he had food and loving attention. Her apartment didn't allow pets, and Eva was allergic to dogs and cats anyway. She had fallen in love with Popsicle even before she fell in love with Alex.

She brooded like that for the next two hours, eating handfuls of dry cereal and cuddling Popsicle on the living room couch. When Alex finally returned, he looked glum. "Sorry to keep you waiting," he said. "We lost the patient and I didn't want to just cut and run."

"It's okay," Nataliya said. Alex sat down next to her on the couch and leaned over to kiss her. Nataliya pulled away.

"Oh my god, seriously, Nataliya?"

"I'm sorry. And I know it's terrible timing. But I can't lie to you. And I can't let you think that this was something that it's not." Nataliya swallowed hard, not wanting to look him in the eye.

Popsicle, sensing the tension, jumped down from the couch and tried to wedge himself underneath it. When he realized he was too fat, he pulled back out and streaked out of the room.

Alex moved to sit on the coffee table and glared at her. "Then what was it?"

"A very, very serious and stupid mistake," she said.

Alex dropped his head in his hands. "Why did you come here, then? You never wanted to get back with me."

"I'm very sorry, Alex. You didn't deserve this. I guess I've been lonely without you, and kissing you reminded me of the good things we did have. I was so caught up." She shook her head. "Work has me exhausted. I'm still adjusting to everything there, learning how to get involved with criminal investigations. Learning how to compartmentalize my life. I'm not very good at that yet. And being with you was easy. Like an old habit. And you've always been good to me in that regard." She sighed. "I didn't mean for this to be a one-night stand. Though I suppose it can't be considered that either. We have too much history."

"So this is it." He looked up at her. "Your one last hurrah."

"That's not what it was," Nataliya said, her chest tight.

Alex shook his head. "It's fine if it was. I won't bother you again. I know I hurt you. But this was really unfair."

"I know. I'm sorry. For what it's worth, I loved you. A lot. But that's not enough. We have different goals. And that's okay."

He didn't reply. She stood up, grabbed her shoes and purse and let herself out of his house. Alex always hid how he felt. He wasn't going to let heartbreak stop him from his life, but she knew he would carry this for a while. For all his narcissism and single-minded career-oriented self, she'd fallen in love with him for a reason. It was just a shame that he couldn't understand.

Beck had a splitting headache. Aspirin didn't do much for him anymore, and he'd quit taking it in fear that it would bore a hole through his stomach. He knew the problem was that he got blasted drunk almost every night, not that the headache was too bad for aspirin to touch it. But he wasn't about to stop drinking. Drinking made him forget. Aspirin did nothing.

He climbed out of his car, his sunglasses thankfully taking most of the insistent sunshine. His stomach rolled at the smell of something he couldn't identify. He was on the SLU campus, so he didn't really want to know what he was smelling. He walked up to the dorm, drawing more than one curious look from young college students who were inexplicably awake at 8 AM on the day after Halloween. He wouldn't be awake either, but he had to interview Jamie Ingle's roommate.

Julie climbed out of the passenger side. "Next time, let me drive," she said, her irritation evident.

He didn't answer. She'd left to go to her office after they connected the two murder victims, but he had returned to the pub to find Patrick and Nataliya both gone. That had been curious, but a text message from his friend soon told him that Nataliya had met up with someone and Patrick went home. Not a man to let a good night go to waste, he opened his own tab and got blistering drunk.

It was probably not wise when he knew they had to go interview Jame Ingle's roommate Katelyn the next day, but he wasn't known as a wise man.

Beck and Julie walked into the dorm building and showed their IDs to the kid manning the front desk. He couldn't be more than twenty, and seeing the badges made him turn pale.

"We're looking for Katelyn Philips," Julie said. "She's aware that we're coming to see her."

"Um, okay, I guess."

The young man was cut off by a young woman leaving the elevator. "I'm here, Dustin, don't worry about it." She managed a weak smile. Beck noticed she was very tiny, probably not even five feet tall, and she wore a school hoodie over jeans and flip flops.

"Katelyn Phillips?" Beck asked. At her nod, he introduced himself. "I'm Detective Beck. This is Special Agent Lyons."

Katelyn looked at Julie much longer than she looked at Beck. That was normal. It wasn't often that a college student talked to the FBI.

"Do you want to talk in the common room?" Katelyn asked.

"Actually, we'd like to take a look at Jamie's room if we could," Beck said.

The girl looked a bit startled, but she nodded. "Okay." She led them to the elevator and pressed the button for the fourth floor. "I'm sorry for the mess in my room. It's been a difficult week, with Jamie missing and our exams and everything."

"Don't worry about it," Julie said. "We've both been to college."

When they reached her floor, Katelyn led them down the hall and into her room. It wasn't as messy as Katelyn had led them to believe. Most of the clutter was discarded clothing and textbooks stacked on the floor.

"That's Jamie's side," Katelyn said, gesturing to the left side of the room. Jamie had black sheets and what looked to be a home made blue and red quilt on top. She had a few posters on her walls, some bands Beck hadn't heard of, a movie poster for *Requiem for a Dream*, and a stack of fantasy novels on her bedside table. There was a coffee maker on top of the mini fridge between the two beds. Her little desk had a closed laptop, several notebooks, and other school supplies. "She's—she was a great roommate. She never bothered me at night so I tried to return the favor. Neither of us brought dates home. She'd bring me food if I was busy studying. I can't believe this happened to her. She wouldn't hurt anyone."

"What was she studying?" Beck asked.

"Psychology. She wanted to join the FBI, actually. Like *Criminal Minds*."

Beck and Julie shared a look. Julie was professional enough not to snort, but Beck knew it was in her, deep within. It wasn't funny, not really, but Beck knew the likelihood of anyone making it to the Behavior Analysis Unit.

"Did she talk about a guy lately? Or say that she'd met anyone? Or that someone was bothering her?" Julie asked.

Katelyn shrugged. "I mean, guys asked her out a lot. She was really outgoing so I guess people were attracted to that. She hasn't dated anyone since we started here in August. Or at least anyone that she told me about. As far as I know, all she did was study and go to class. I didn't even know she left campus Sunday night."

"When did she leave the room?" Beck asked.

"I'm sorry, I have no idea. I went home for the weekend. My mom's birthday." Katelyn let out a sigh. "She texted me a couple times, mostly just checking that I made it safely and asking when I'd be back. I told her Sunday night, probably close to 10:00 PM. It's a long drive from Milwaukee."

"When did she send her last text?" Beck asked.

"Six. I'd already left by then, so I wasn't able to reply until like an hour later when I stopped for gas."

"Do you know if there was anything going on that would have interested her enough to leave campus alone?" Beck was beginning to get a bit frustrated. It wasn't Katelyn's fault that she didn't know anything. He hoped that by looking through Jamie's laptop they'd find more information.

"I don't know, probably not. She might have left with one of her other friends. She was outgoing, as I said, so she always had someone to go out with."

Beck walked over to the laptop and opened the lid with the cuff of his coat. He probably didn't need to worry about fingerprints since it was highly unlikely that whoever raped Jamie had messed with it. Regardless, they'd have someone process Jamie's half of the room. The laptop was turned on, but it was password protected.

"Do you happen to know her password?" he asked.

"Um, yeah, actually. She gave it to me in case something happened to her. I thought that was weird, but I didn't think much of it." Katelyn went to her desk and wrote something on a sticky note. She handed it to Beck, who typed it in, again with his finger covered. He logged in and saw that the desktop wallpaper was that creepy eye from the Requiem for a Dream poster.

"She liked that movie, huh?" he asked.

"I guess so. She never watched it when I was in the room." Katelyn shrugged.

"Could you get us the name of some of her friends?" Julie asked while Beck tinkered around on the computer. He opened her email, but it was all school-related stuff.

Katelyn wrote them all down as he closed the laptop. "This is going to be too much to go through now," he said to Julie. "I'll have someone come and process everything."

Julie nodded. After a moment, Katelyn handed Beck a piece of paper with several students' names on it along with their phone numbers and dorms. She must have pulled them from her phone while he was messing around. "You didn't happen to find her cell phone in the room, did you?" Beck asked.

Katelyn shook her head.

"All right. Well, thank you for your time. If you can think of anything, please give us a call." Julie handed her a card. Beck fumbled in his pocket and handed her one as well.

"I hope you can figure out what happened to her," Katelyn said. "It's got the rest of us here spooked. It happened close enough to campus that everyone's afraid to go out alone."

"That's not a bad idea," Julie said. "Keep aware of your surroundings, trust your gut. And it's not always strangers that can hurt you."

Katelyn's eyes widened. "Do you think someone she knew did this to her?"

Beck raised an eyebrow at Julie. That was certainly nowhere in the investigation, and the odd series of events that connected Jamie Ingle with the girl in Alton seemed to suggest a random rapist more than anything else. "We can't comment on the investigation further," Julie said. "I just want to make sure you and the other students stay safe."

"Okay," Katelyn said, but she didn't look convinced.

"We'll have a couple of uniforms here within a half hour to gather Jamie's things," Beck said.

Katelyn nodded and escorted them the two steps to the door.

"Well," Julie said when they were in the elevator. "Do you want to divide and conquer this list?"

"Not particularly, but you're going to make me anyway, aren't you?"

Julie gave him a grin. "Sucks to be hungover, doesn't it?"

CHAPTER SIX

"Do you think they were murdered?"

Her question seemed to surprise Patrick. They stood at the front desk of the police station in Alton. They would have had mountains of paperwork just to get the body transported over state lines, not to mention the girl had already been buried and that would cause even more paperwork and a court order. Agent Lyons didn't want to deal with it. Instead, on Tuesday Nataliya and Patrick had driven across the river to Alton to meet with the medical examiner.

"You know I can't say one way or the other," Patrick replied.

Nataliya knew that, but she also felt like he was hiding something. He'd been distant all day. Not rude, just preoccupied.

"I'm so sorry."

They both looked over at the new voice. A young man in a suit had appeared behind the desk. "Dr. Feigle isn't in today."

"I thought Special Agent Lyons set up this meeting specifically," Dr. Morana said.

The young man shrugged. "I'm sorry. I don't know anything about that. He did leave this for you." He handed over a manila envelope. It had Dr. Morana's name on it. "I can let him know you came by."

"Thank you," Dr. Morana said, a bit curtly. "Come on, Dr. Vasilyeva." He left the building, Nataliya following closely. Once they were back in his car, he opened the envelope and pulled out a thick sheaf of paper. "He gave us the autopsy report and his personal notes."

"That's better than nothing, I guess," Nataliya said. "Maybe he's sick?"

Dr. Morana sighed. "Maybe. He could have just emailed them. Saved us a trip." He pulled out of the parking lot and headed back toward the interstate.

Nataliya couldn't disagree. She'd never been to Alton before, but she once heard stories that it was supposedly one of the most haunted places in the US. "Have you ever been on a ghost tour?" she asked, pointing at a billboard advertising Alton as *the Most Haunted Small Town in the USA*. She supposed it was a decent tourist attraction, if one were into such things.

Dr. Morana scoffed. "No. It's ridiculous. They're simply exploiting the fact that Alton housed Confederate prisoners of war and was a stop on the Underground Railroad. The tourism board says there are a few racist ghosts and some slaves who never made it to freedom, then they'll grab a wad of cash from bored tourists who came home to visit their in-laws or didn't want to drive for one of the St. Louis ghost tours and then call it a night."

Nataliya fought the urge to chuckle. "I didn't think so. It seems macabre."

"Some people say that about our profession." He gave her a sidelong glance, complete with a half-smirk. He was usually so stoic that it was a bit charming to see his more playful side.

"We're not exploiting escaped slaves," she pointed out.

That made him laugh, and she grinned. "You're not wrong," he said. "In any case, I think it's all foolish. Maybe it's just a backdrop to talking about real history, but the fact is they're perpetuating a lie."

"What if they don't think it's a lie? I don't really believe in ghosts, but some people are absolutely convinced."

"Doesn't change the fact that it's not true." Dr. Morana let out a sigh. "I guess I'm not a total skeptic. Don't get me wrong, I don't think people are stupid for their beliefs. I just think that it can be dangerous to play with things you don't understand."

"Like Ouija boards?"

He didn't say anything for a long time as he concentrated on driving back to the interstate. When they merged into westbound traffic, he finally replied, "I guess so. I don't know anything about them. I just wish that people would let the dead rest." His earlier joking tone turned serious. "You'll see what I mean as you work in this job more. People are so obsessed with death because our culture doesn't really understand it. It's a taboo. How many times have I seen someone unable to grieve? They just shut down. So many people, men in particular, aren't allowed to show their mourning. It's practically criminal. Cultures like Mexico have Dia de los Muertos, many Asian cultures pray to their ancestors, Hindus believe in reincarnation. To them, death isn't the final destination in the grand scheme of things. Even Christianity has heaven and hell. But so many people are afraid of the oblivion that comes after. Or so they assume comes after. So they invent a fairy tale and try to communicate with those who have passed. And I have to watch so many people unable to process death. Instead of letting people die, go on, and mourning properly, they come up with ghost stories to convince themselves that it's not the end."

Nataliya didn't quite know what to say to that. Her parents were raised in Soviet Russia, and they had no religion. They were tentative Orthodox Church goers when they came to America soon after her birth and not too long after the Soviet Union collapsed, but they didn't really press the issue with her. It was as if they were still afraid to show some belief in a supreme being. "I agree with you that our culture doesn't know how to mourn the dead. I just don't know if everyone is making up a ghost story to make themselves feel better. Some people have unexplained experiences."

"Yeah, I suppose you're right. I can be pretty passionate about this topic." He shot her an apologetic smile. "I didn't mean to upset you."

"Not at all, I'm glad you shared that with me. I'm still trying to figure out how to approach all of this, and how to communicate with grieving families," she said. "So I take it you're not afraid of the Grim Reaper?"

He let out a cackle, and that startled her so badly she nearly jumped in her seat. "What the hell was that about?" she asked, her eyes wide.

"Nothing, sorry. Sorry."

They were quiet for a while longer. Nataliya didn't want to press. She still didn't know what was so funny about her question. She was afraid of dying, not necessarily out of fear of what came after, but of leaving a life unfinished. However, she was certain that Dr. Morana wasn't talking about that type of fear of death.

"Hey, can you stop for coffee soon?" Nataliya asked. "I didn't grab any before we left."

"You drink more coffee than anyone else I've ever met."

"It got me through medical school. And my residency, for that matter. Most likely because quitting cold turkey meant I'd be in withdrawal. I reached the point where I need a ton in order for it to have any effect on me."

"Fine, fine. We'll stop for your liquid drugs." His good humor seemed firmly back in place, and for that she was thankful. She liked him a lot more when he was like this. He was always so reserved, even with Denise and the other doctors at the morgue. It felt much more natural for him to joke around and tease her. She understood that he had to cultivate a certain image for his job, but that didn't mean he always had to be Mr. Serious.

Patrick read through the autopsy report for the fifth time. The Alton victim had eaten a very specific assortment of organic items before her death. He wrote each of them down in a notebook. Agent Lyons was pushing through all the various tests on Jamie Ingle's blood and stomach contents, but it'd still take time. He glanced over at Nataliya. She was sipping the iced coffee he'd bought for her before they returned to the morgue. It seemed too cold outside for iced coffee, but he didn't dare say a word. She flipped through previous autopsy reports that he wanted her to look at. She had to know how to detail many different deaths, and the best way for her to learn was to see actual reports.

He looked back at the Alton victim's report. Her name had been Rachel Merrick. The photos of her dead body showed that she had short, blonde hair. She didn't look much like Jamie Ingle from what he could tell. The photos of her heart, along with the coroner's description, perfectly matched the one in Jamie Ingle's chest. Collapsed, squeezed as if it were nothing more than a hunk of clay. She was a year older than Jamie Ingle, and she had taken a break from college to travel as an actress on a riverboat. It appeared the police department had included everything they had on her. She was originally from Kansas City, and she had gone missing on the riverboat's stop in Alton. When Rachel hadn't shown up for her scheduled call time for their show, her boss immediately alerted the authorities. Even before they could officially declare her a missing person, her body was found on the far end of the town. Her skirt had been pushed up to her waist, her T-shirt had been ripped open, and her bra slashed. Just like Jamie Ingle. Her death was determined to be a result of a heart defect, though there was an open investigation on her rape.

"So this guy was strangled, but that's not what killed him?"

Patrick glanced at Nataliya, who was studying an autopsy report intently. "What?"

"This autopsy report. Dr. Paulson performed it. He was strangled, but the cause of death was a brain hemorrhage."

"What about it?"

Nataliya studied him for a moment then shook her head. "Never mind, I'll ask Dr. Paulson when she gets in this afternoon. You're busy."

Patrick blinked and shrugged. He went back to studying the case file on Rachel Merrick. Something struck him as odd, but he couldn't put his finger on it. He really wished he could have spoken to someone involved in the case. The Alton PD had no interest in talking to him either, and he hoped Julie was having better luck than he was. He knew he wasn't technically a detective and he was simply supposed to do an autopsy and present the facts, but his interest in the case was more than just happenstance.

His conversation with Nataliya on the drive back had also put him off-kilter. It wasn't that he didn't believe in ghosts. It was that they weren't what most people thought. Nataliya seemed satisfied with their conversation, but he felt frustrated over keeping it quiet. Most people didn't bother to ask him such questions. Beck sure as hell didn't. And Patrick didn't have many friends. In fact, Beck was pretty much it. Patrick wouldn't consider his colleagues friends, and most other people he was just acquaintances with. A deep abiding friendship? That was a difficult thing for him. They'd start to notice that he wasn't exactly normal.

A knock on the door interrupted his thoughts. Dr. Paulson walked in without waiting. She was in her late thirties, and unlike Dr. Hammond, she had some negativity surrounding the fact that her boss was younger than her. She got over it after a while, but he still sensed a frosty attitude from her most of the time. "The printer *finally* got them done."

"What?" He looked at her in complete confusion.

She rolled her eyes and slapped a card on his desk. "The wedding invitations," she said. "Remember, the printer screwed them up, twice? How can I have people come to my wedding if they were told the wrong date?"

"Oh! Right, I'm sorry. Of course." Patrick picked up the card. It was embossed and had fancy golden filigree design all over it. In elaborate calligraphy, it read:

With great pleasure
Dr. Adriana Paulson
and
Dr. Jose Delgado
invite you to join them
at the celebration of their marriage

Saturday the sixteenth of December
at six-thirty in the evening
The Coronado - Ballroom
St. Louis, Missouri
Black tie preferred

"Black tie, Adriana? Really?" Patrick shook his head.

"I wanted black tie required, but some people can't afford to rent a tux, I guess." Dr. Paulson sounded slightly irritated, but she didn't let it show on her face.

Patrick didn't want to comment on his colleague's perception of people's socioeconomic statuses. "Don't worry, I'll wear one."

"You'd better." Adriana smiled in a way that told him she honestly didn't care one way or another. "Oh! Nataliya!" She hurried over to the other desk and handed Nataliya an invitation. "I know we don't know each other very well, but I'd love it if you could make it to my wedding."

"Wow, thank you." Nataliya looked it over. "This looks like it's going to be quite an event!"

"I've only been dreaming about my wedding since I was a little girl." Adriana laughed. "You'll love Jose, everyone does."

"She's right," Patrick interrupted. "He's the kindest person you'll ever meet."

Nataliya glanced both of them and set the invitation on the desk. "I think I have that weekend free. I'm going back home the week after for Christmas."

"Wonderful!" Adriana gave her a nod and left the room as quickly as she came in.

Nataliya went back to perusing the notes and Patrick cleared his throat.

"What?" she asked.

"Didn't you have a question for her?"

Nataliya bit her lip. "I thought you weren't paying attention."

He gave her a pointed look. A moment later she seemed to realize what he meant, and she launched out of her chair after Dr. Paulson. He shook his head and went back to the autopsy report. Nataliya was trying so hard to figure him out. If he wasn't careful, she eventually might.

CHAPTER SEVEN

The days passed in a haze of autopsies, crime scenes, and even one notable instance where Nataliya tagged along with Patrick as he testified in a court hearing. She soaked it all in, making her own notes on her day-to-day activities in addition to the piles of paperwork she had to do for each autopsy and case on which she assisted. She worked with Dr. Morana most of the time, but once or twice she worked with Dr. Hammond or Adriana. She hadn't heard anything more on the odd case of the girls with the collapsed heart, and her intense curiosity never waned.

One day, she was deep cleaning the autopsy exam room in a fit of energy and irritation. The dead body smell wasn't going away. It was Thursday, not the usual day for a deep clean. It was also just over a week until Adriana's wedding, and the weather had turned bitingly cold.

Patrick walked into the room and looked confused to see her scrubbing the exam table. "Was the table dirty or something?" he asked.

"I don't know, I keep smelling this room and it's driving me nuts."

"Oh yeah, sometimes that happens to me too. It gets stuck in your nose and you just want to smell nothing but cleaning chemicals for a while." Patrick shrugged. "Maybe you should get fresh air next time. Nothing like the bracing freezing weather after a thaw in St. Louis to invigorate the senses."

"Maybe," she replied, standing up straight. The table was as clean as it would ever get.

"Well, here's your chance, though not a very good one, I'm afraid. Beck called. We need to go to a crime scene in Forest Park."

"All right." Nataliya put the cleaning tools away and grabbed her heavy coat. Bundling up always seemed a chore. Her mother sent her innumerable hats and scarves and shawls, all knitted by hand. It was a thoughtful gesture, and Nataliya was thankful for them when winter hit full force. Leave it to a mother raised in Russia to endow her child with multiple warmth items. St. Louis never got as cold as Minnesota, at least.

"Ready?" Patrick asked when Nataliya left the building. She grunted her assent and climbed into the passenger seat of his car.

"What are the details?" she asked, buckling up.

"Not sure yet. Beck said it was bad, though. He wanted me to come in fresh."

Nataliya played with the fingers of her gloves during the drive. It wasn't too far, but Forest Park was huge. She wondered which part they were going to. She didn't bother to ask, feeling too cold to make conversation. Patrick's car took forever to heat up. He drove past the zoo, which looked busy in spite of the cold weather and the fact that it was a school day, and stopped in front of a heavily wooded area. Several police cars, an ambulance, and a crowd of onlookers told Nataliya where the body had been found. Patrick pulled up alongside a police car, ignoring cars trying to find a spot for the zoo, and held up his ID lanyard to the police. He got out of the car, and she scrambled out after him. Nataliya fumbled as she tried to pull her lanyard from under her scarf and coat.

"The coroner's here," one officer said, lifting the tape for them to duck under.

Beck stood with Julie at the edge of the trees. "Hey," he said when they got close. "It's bad."

Patrick and Nataliya exchanged a look. "I've seen worse," Patrick said in all confidence, and Nataliya believed him.

"I know, but she might not have." Beck nodded at Nataliya.

Patrick ignored him and walked into the trees and Nataliya saw one of the CSU people photographing the body. When she got closer, she realized that the body was half covered by fallen leaves. It didn't look quite right.

It hit her that it had been raining for several days straight in unseasonably warm weather before it turned freezing. The body was bloated, and parts of the skin had split from the gases. The water did no favors to the corpse. Patrick waved off the CSU and squatted down next to the body. Nataliya took a couple of steps and was immediately hit with the smell. The one she'd been trying to eradicate from the exam room.

Her stomach roiled, and she bolted. She raced over to the crime scene tape and vomited just past it. She fell to her knees as she coughed and spit. Her eyes watered and her stomach continued to heave. It was painful. She also felt a flare of anger. Nataliya had never once gotten nauseated during medical school or her residency. Her iron stomach had been her pride, and it was part of why she'd been selected for the Forensic Pathology Fellowship. And now she'd embarrassed herself in front of her boss and a good amount of both the St. Louis Police Department and the Forest Park Ranger Service.

"Nataliya! Are you okay?"

She looked up and saw Patrick had come after her. "I'm fine," she said, wishing she could brush her teeth. "I guess the smell was too much for once. I feel like an idiot."

Patrick didn't say anything, just crouched down next to her and put a hand on her shoulder. "Sometimes seeing the bodies out here, like this, it's difficult."

"I was fine with Jamie Ingle."

"But she wasn't in bloat."

Nataliya didn't know what to say. A ranger came by and offered her a bottle of water. She took it. She swished a mouthful around and spit it out. She then drank deeply.

"I'm fine," she said finally. She stood up, thankful that she didn't need Patrick to help her. Steeling herself for the smell, she walked back toward the body. She put her scarf over her nose, no longer caring if the cops thought she couldn't hold her stomach.

Patrick shook his head. "I can't tell anything other than the body is female. We're going to need to open her up."

Beck had come forward at some point. "When do you think you can do that?"

"As soon as the body arrives at the morgue," Patrick said. "Just for you Beck."

"It's what I always wanted," Beck said, his sarcasm thick. "You all right, Nataliya?"

"I'm fine," she said, though she wasn't.

"If it makes you feel any better, both Grainger and Stahl puked too."

Strangely, it did. Even though she had no idea who Grainger and Stahl were.

"My guess is that the rain kept the smell down somewhat," Patrick said. "No one was parking this far out for the zoo with the constant downpour. It's hard to tell how many days the body has been out here due to the rain affecting the decomposition. I'll be able to find out more at the morgue."

"I would have thought it was just a jogger with a heart attack, except for her clothes," Beck said.

Nataliya hadn't even noticed the clothing, the body's grotesque bloat had been so searing. A strip of black fabric that might have once been a skirt twisted around the body's waist. The shirt was open down the front, and the brown staining made it hard to determine the original color. No bra, or at least not one she could see.

"Like the other two," Julie said, sidling up to Beck. "Which is why I'm here."

"Damn," Patrick said. He turned away from the body. "Another one."

"If the heart is like the others, then something really fucking weird is going on." Beck shook his head. "Two is a coincidence, three is a pattern."

"No need to borrow trouble yet," Patrick told him. "I still have to do the autopsy."

"No ID on this one either," Julie said, "which is going to make this harder."

Patrick let out a sigh, and Nataliya might have done the same, but she felt as if she could scarcely breathe through the scarf. Though that meant she couldn't inhale the rot smell. "Yeah," he said after a long moment. "After CSU is done, get the transporters in. This autopsy gets priority." He nodded at both Beck and Julie and walked back to the car.

"He seems terser than usual," Julie commented.

"We've both been in a funk," Nataliya said. "Maybe it's the weather."

"Everyone's in a funk," Beck interrupted before Julie could say anything. "Damn seasonal depression. You'd better go catch up. Have Patrick call me when he has his COD."

"Sure." Nataliya ran after Patrick, thankful that the rotting smell was replaced by the sharp cold of 22 degrees Fahrenheit air. The Caw-caw! of a crow got her attention. In a tree right by the sidewalk, she saw four crows that looked as if they were waiting for the humans to leave so they could feast on the carrion. Her stomach rolled again.

When they started the autopsy a couple of hours later, Nataliya felt even sicker than before. She sprayed her face mask with perfume she borrowed from Denise. It helped a bit, though the perfume was sickeningly sweet. The difference was it didn't make her want to throw up like the corpse smell did.

"You look pale," Patrick said, though she didn't know how he could tell when he could only see her eyes.

"I guess I was not prepared for this."

"It takes time to get used to," he admitted. He put on his own mask and face shield. Working with a decomposing body at this level could be messy, she knew.

"How long did it take for you to get used to bodies like this?"

He didn't answer her. Patrick turned on the video camera and began the autopsy as usual. Nataliya felt a bit quivery as she watched him cut open the decaying flesh. "Don't be surprised if there are maggots and larvae," he said. "We'll be taking specimens for those too. Rick, one of the CSU, gathered some at the crime scene."

"He's the forensic entomologist, right?" Nataliya was grateful that she remembered that much. The smells were a powerful distraction.

Patrick nodded. He continued with the autopsy, noting the levels of decay, where the skin had ruptured or was still bloated. He spoke aloud for the camera. "The body is too decomposed to determine sexual assault. The rain hampered some of the presence of maggots, but we've taken several specimens."

Well, Nataliya took them. She grabbed the maggots with her tweezers and put them in different containers, each marked with a detailed label.

Patrick then opened the rib cage. It was disgusting work, much worse than on a fresh corpse. After he set the sternum aside and examined the lungs, he retrieved the heart.

"Collapsed," Nataliya said. "Decomposition didn't do that."

Patrick let out a heavy sigh. "It's exactly like the other two girls." He set the heart aside. "Based on the level of decay and the rainfall, I'd say she died five days ago."

Nataliya looked down at the assemblage. The girl, woman, whoever she was, couldn't be identified as she currently was. Beck and his people would be sifting through missing persons reports. Though it was December, Forest Park had a huge tourist draw due to the zoo and the art museum. They'd taken X-rays of her body, in case they needed dental records, and tissue samples for tests. Tox screens, blood, DNA, anything they could. The other two victims didn't have any sort of drugs or alcohol in their systems. Just the weird mix of herbs in their stomach contents. Nataliya had collected this unknown woman's stomach contents as well, but she knew what they were going to be.

"Pat—" She didn't finish her thought as a heave went through her body. To avoid throwing up in her mask, she darted out the door, ripping it off as she went. She gasped in the clean air in the hallway. Remembering what he said earlier about fresh air, she went outside and sat on the sidewalk stoop, feeling sorry for herself. The cold air made her more aware of what she'd just done. Not only had she started to call her boss by his first name, but she ran out in the middle of an autopsy. What was wrong with her? The smell wasn't that bad, and she'd gotten used to the sight of the putrefaction. She knew she'd be able to handle it before too long. And now she'd made a fool out of herself in front of Dr. Morana, twice.

He didn't come after her, which was hardly a surprise. He couldn't stop in the middle of an autopsy for a criminal investigation just to make sure his little mentee was okay. No one else in the morgue had even seen her. She took the moment alone to collect herself. The cold air was making her shiver, so she stood up and started pacing. Finally, the nausea abated. At least she hadn't thrown up this time. After she felt much more stable and her knees stopped shaking, she went back into the morgue. She found Patrick still working on the autopsy. He was poking around the dead woman's brain, like he was used to rotting bodies every day. Well, he probably was. He had been the coroner for a while, and a medical examiner even longer than that. He didn't even look up when she came back in, as he was busy giving notes to the camera.

When he took a break, she apologized in a quiet voice.

"Don't worry about it," Dr. Morana said in a voice that didn't feel very sincere.

"I'll do better next time, I promise."

"I know you will, Nataliya. It's really okay. You didn't throw up on the corpse, did you?" She couldn't see his mouth behind the mask, but she figured he was smirking. "And besides, this is not a pretty body to look at."

"I know. But I'm supposed to be a professional."

Dr. Morana shrugged as if he didn't know what to say to that. He started putting the organs back. Stitching the body back was not wise with how easily the skin split, but he moved with a practiced ease, putting the body back together in interesting ways. She helped him put the body into the cooler.

"Okay," she said, once he turned off the camera. "You go transcribe that. I'm going to clean the shit out of this room."

Dr. Morana had taken off his mask, and this time he did smirk. "Have fun." He left with the SD card from the camera in his hand. Nataliya didn't care if he thought she was silly. She was going to clean the morgue as many times as it took until she didn't feel like she was going to slip in corpse juice.

CHAPTER EIGHT

"The second Jane Doe is Amelia Croft. Age twenty. She's been missing for over a year. Her brother thought she ran off with a boyfriend."

Patrick listened to Beck on speakerphone. Beck had gotten the DNA results before he did, which was hardly a surprise. All Patrick needed to know next was where to send the body for mortuary services. He fiddled with the zipper on his hoodie. He had to get ready for Adriana's wedding. Beck was going too, but he was working overtime to close the Jane Doe case.

"The only reason we even found her identity is because her brother was in the database from a DUI and the DNA was enough of a match to ping." Beck sighed.

"So she'd been missing for a while, doing whatever she was doing, before she died." Patrick got up from his couch and went to rifle through his closet for the tux he'd had to wear to some awards ceremony years ago for the city. He didn't remember why he'd even gone, but he'd bought the tuxedo on a whim. He didn't normally buy a lot of fancy clothing, but he thought he looked good in it. And then he never wore it again.

"Yeah. She didn't have any sort of record, but that doesn't mean anything. Just like the other two. This is the most bizarre case I've ever worked on. I'm used to gang violence and stupid college kids driving drunk. Not this. Julie said she saw some weird stuff back in New York, so I guess she isn't as bothered. She's juggling three other cases too so she's letting me handle most of it. It seems St. Louis isn't a high priority for the FBI."

Patrick had seen something more bizarre than Julie, but he wasn't about to tell Beck that. "Shouldn't you be getting ready for the wedding?" he asked, pulling out the tux and crouching down to find his nice shoes.

"I still find it weird that she invited me and Agent Lyons," Beck said, not answering the question. "Doesn't she have any friends?"

"I think she wanted to fill the ballroom to make the pictures look more impressive. I don't know. But she's going to have great food and great alcohol. Try to be nice, okay? She's been looking forward to this for so long."

"Look, I shaved for her. I won't get too smashed. It's her wedding. I just feel awkward."

Patrick couldn't argue with that. He might have felt awkward in Beck's position too. As it was, Patrick didn't get invited to many weddings. He'd only been to one before, and that was in medical school. "You'll have to update me on the rest of the case later. I'm picking up Nataliya before the wedding."

"Oh right, she's going too. Why are you driving her?"

"She's been having dizzy spells lately and she said she doesn't want to try to drive in midtown in an evening gown."

"Dizzy spells?"

"Yeah, she said working at the morgue has been a lot more stressful than she originally thought and she hasn't been eating well. I think she just needs more time to adjust. She hasn't even worked there two whole months yet."

Beck sighed. "She's a good kid but she's got a lot of learning coming."

"We all start from somewhere," Patrick said.

"Except you. I think you came out a perfectly formed adult. All right, I'll see you at the wedding. Make sure you look pretty for your Russian lady."

"My Russian lady?"

Beck snickered and hung up. Patrick frowned. Sure, he thought Nataliya was beautiful and had exactly the right attitude for his line of work, but his? Beck was being irritating.

Patrick put the call out of his mind and took a quick shower. Though he knew he probably smelled fine, some of Nataliya's anxieties about smells had rubbed off on him. He'd had to physically stop her from deep cleaning the entire morgue again. She was already exhausted, and he didn't want her to hurt herself. A beautiful night at a friend's wedding would be exactly what they both needed. No murders, no black magic, just amazing food, dancing, and cocktails.

He wasn't a party animal by any stretch, but he was desperately wanting a distraction. The fact that he couldn't figure out how to present the recent string of murders to Beck in a rational fashion was bugging him. He knew he had to find whoever was killing these girls, but he had no idea how. He was trained as a forensic pathologist, not a magical private investigator.

When he got out of the shower, he toweled off and got dressed. A thought struck him as he went over the cases in his mind yet again. The herbs in their stomachs weren't a coincidence either. He ran into his office and grabbed a book off his shelf.

Spells and Incantations by Rufus Whitecrow. It was a handsome, leather-bound volume with an embossed cover displaying all manner of plants, mushrooms, and creepy crawlies.

It had been given to him, long ago. The pages were marked with slips of paper, some showing the spells that were legit. Others were fake. The book was nothing more than someone trying to make a buck off aspiring witches who had no idea how to truly tap into the powers they wanted. From what Patrick could tell, the writer copied a lot of information from other sources, long since past copyright. He'd even mentioned it in his acknowledgments.

He flipped through while standing at the bookshelf. He really needed to finish getting ready, but this couldn't wait. Not if he wanted to finally figure out what had been nagging at him. After reading a half dozen entries, he finally found what he was looking for.

Love Spell

The paper slip that bookmarked the page denoted the love potion as a fake, with absolutely no basis in real magic.

- *A leaf of Ragweed*
- *Three dried Cloves*
- *A pinch of Dill Seeds*
- *A Jasmine blossom*
- *A red Tulip petal*
- *A sprig of Witch Hazel*

Combine these in a mortar and pestle and add to food or drink that smell and taste strongly. The object of your affection will return your desire and love thrice fold. Lasts for up to one week, longer if the subject has a quick digestion. Not recommended for extended use.

Every single one of those ingredients, minus the red tulip and jasmine, was found in the stomach contents of all three victims. And he was sure the red tulip petal and jasmine blossom weren't found because the tests didn't know to look for them. Someone had read this book and wanted to get the girls to love him. Most likely it was a man, based on the manner of the murders.

Rufus Whitecrow must have gotten his inspiration from the meaning of flowers, because all of those plants had something to do with love or faithfulness. Patrick didn't have time to look into Rufus Whitecrow now, but he had a feeling the man had either written the book for entertainment purposes only, or he had gotten a kick out of someone mashing together random plants and trying to slip them to people like a supernatural roofie.

Patrick set the book on his desk and hurried out of the room. He had to go pick up Nataliya. His suspicions could wait.

Nataliya struggled to get her high heel on as she staggered toward the door. Dr. Morana was right on time, but she was not. Her beautiful dress didn't seem to fit quite right, and she'd had to find a waist shaper to force her already slim waist into the dramatic black evening gown she'd bought for the occasion. She didn't know when she'd started to bloat a bit, but it was frustrating nonetheless. No doubt it was connected to her exhaustion and dizziness. Nataliya had always been healthy, exercising when she could and trying to be a positive person, but for a formal black-tie wedding, her normally carefree attitude toward her body was scarce. She'd fallen in love with the thin-strapped black velvet dress, with blue Swarovski crystals sewn in a spray from the waist. The neckline plunged a bit low, but she didn't feel overly exposed as she wasn't entirely well-endowed. And thankfully the waist cincher worked, smooshing her back to her usual shape. The shoes didn't feel right, but heels never felt right.

She threw open the door to her apartment and bent over to pull her shoe all the way on. "Hold on, I need to grab my purse."

Dr. Morana didn't say anything as she hurried back into the kitchen, her heels pounding against the floor. The people who lived in the apartment below were not going to be happy, but at least it wasn't late. She grabbed her purse and the fancy gift she'd purchased from the registry. She'd been nervous about what kind of gifts that Dr. Paulson would ask for, considering the formal ceremony, but it had been surprisingly affordable. Patrick told her it was because several of Adriana's students were coming to the wedding as well, and she knew none of them would be able to afford anything.

She came back to the door where Dr. Morana waited, the door still open

Eva strode in, her nurse-on-a-mission expression squarely in place.

"Move it, Undertaker," she said, shouldering Dr. Morana aside. She shed clothes as she stormed by until she was just in her scrubs.

"She knows I'm not a mortician, right?" Dr. Morana asked Nataliya.

Nataliya fought the urge to chuckle. "She knows."

They heard Eva rustling around in the kitchen, swearing. "We'd better leave before she comes back and takes out all her doctor-fueled frustration on us." Nataliya grabbed his arm and pulled him towards the door.

"You look great by the—whoa!"

Nataliya tugged him out of the door and shut it behind her. "Trust me, we should get going."

Dr. Morana looked concerned but thankfully didn't say anything. He helped her down the steps from her door and to the car. He even opened her door for her, which she thought was charming. She wore a silvery shawl over her dress, but it wasn't doing much for the freezing air.

"Your roommate is a nurse, right?"

"ER nurse," Nataliya said. "She works with one doctor in particular who treats nurses as his personal servants, and she's just itching for the day when she gets put on a different rotation."

"Say no more," Dr. Morana said. It was pretty well known, even among doctors themselves, how some of them treated the nurses.

The ride to the Coronado was uneventful, with the two of them just talking about what they'd bought for Dr. Paulson and Jose. Nataliya still had yet to meet the amazing Jose, and she looked forward to seeing what all the fuss was about. The Coronado had valet parking, which Dr. Morana seemed uncomfortable about. Though he was stunning in his tuxedo and with his hair neatly combed, he looked strange in the finery. Nataliya had never seen him in such a situation, working with him day in and day out in their autopsy gowns and sitting at their office desks in business attire.

Dr. Morana offered his arm to her, and she took it. She fought back a girly giggle. The Coronado was an amazing place, and she was glad she'd gone for the fancier dress even though it was more expensive. She'd never thought a forensic pathology fellowship would lead her to attending a black-tie wedding on the arm of her handsome boss. Walking into the venue was like walking into a fairy tale. The 1920s architecture and opulence were a sight for the eyes. The ushers led them to the arrangement of gold wire-backed chairs where several people were already seated. Crystal chandeliers hovered above the guests, casting reflections onto the slatted ceiling. Everything was gold and white, except for the pop of red poinsettias Dr. Paulson had chosen for the ballroom.

They were seated next to Beck and Julie. Beck looked surprisingly clean cut with no facial hair and a well-pressed suit. Julie's gown surprised her. She would have expected the FBI agent to wear some plain black gown, the better to blend in. Instead, she wore a black and gold dress with a trumpet skirt. The art deco design fit in well with the twenties style of the building.

After polite conversation about their dresses, the decor, and the beautiful, soft music being played by a string quartet, the wedding finally started. The priest walked up to the front, along with the groom. Jose was a good-looking man about Adriana Paulson's age. His three groomsmen stood beside him in a line as they waited. The bridal march started playing, and the little flower girl, who looked to be a relative of Jose, strode down the aisle. The ring bearer walked behind her, a boy slightly too old for the job. He managed to rein in his irritated smile as the photographer snapped photos of him. The bridesmaids came down the aisle in gorgeous red dresses that matched the poinsettias they carried. One was visibly pregnant, and it looked as if her dress had been altered to fit her belly. Nataliya was a bit surprised. With the wedding's level of formality, she might have thought that a woman in advanced pregnancy would ruin the "image." She should have known better than to think such a thing. Dr. Paulson had been nothing but kind to her, even inviting her to a wedding so soon after meeting. Adriana cared about her students' budgets and apparently had even paid for the bridesmaid's dresses herself. She wanted a formal wedding, and she didn't want other people to have to sacrifice for it.

Everyone stood when Adriana walked down the aisle. Her dress was magnificent, but Nataliya barely noticed the details. Dr. Paulson looked utterly radiant. She had a small smile on her face as she kept her eyes on her fiancé. She looked completely at peace, like she was doing the exact right thing with no regrets and no anxieties. Nataliya couldn't help but watch her as she walked by, her perfect posture almost second nature. Nataliya thought briefly of Alex. She knew she wouldn't have looked so serene if she'd married him. She didn't remember how the brides had looked at other weddings she'd been to. Usually she looked at their dresses, or the groom's face. Nataliya felt envious. She wanted to look like that, and not just about a man. She wanted to be at peace with herself.

Taking the fellowship at the morgue had been nerve-racking. There wasn't a lot of peace in that decision, even if she knew it was her vocation. Maybe someday she'd find that inner peace.

Dr. Morana took her hand and squeezed it, as if he could hear her thoughts. Before she could think about the impropriety of the action, he let go. It hadn't been inappropriate, but she supposed it could have been construed that way. Everyone sat down, and the ceremony began.

Nataliya hadn't been to a Catholic wedding before, but she had been to both secular and Russian Orthodox weddings. She was glad this was not an Orthodox wedding. She wouldn't be able to sit still for two hours of chanting.

After the traditional vows and the first kiss, everyone was shuffled into the main ballroom while the photographer snapped photos of the wedding party and the families. Beck, Julie, Dr. Morana, and Nataliya had all been seated at the same table. There were five chairs at the table, but one had no name assigned to it.

"This is the fanciest wedding I've ever been to," Beck said, tugging at his tie. "I got married in a barn."

"A barn?" Julie asked, furrowing her brow and wrinkling her nose.

"We grew up in rural Illinois," Beck replied. "It was a thing. And it wasn't a working barn. It was a wedding venue, mostly for rich people who wanted the rustic look." He scoffed. "We weren't rich, but it was cheap enough for us to get married there and have a caterer. God. I was a dumbass."

"Was?" Julie asked, sipping at the ice water that had been served as they waited for dinner to start.

"Shut up." Beck looked longingly at the bar, but it wouldn't open until the bride and groom came in.

Nataliya almost asked where Beck's wife was but then remembered Dr. Morana had told her that Beck was divorcing her. Apparently, the woman had cheated on him. Twice. After the second time, Beck kicked her out, but she was trying to get the house away from him along with alimony. Apparently, she wanted half his pension as well, in spite of the fact that Beck wasn't even thirty-five yet and they'd been married less than ten years.

After what seemed like an eternity, Adriana and Jose were announced, and they walked into the ballroom to whoops and cheers and applause. They took their seats at the wedding party table, and food was served.

"I feel queasy," Nataliya said, shifting in her chair. The waist cincher was not her friend right now. "I think I'm going to stick with water for a bit."

When the waiters came around, everyone else accepted the wine that had been paired with their chosen meal. Nataliya had wanted the beef tips six weeks ago, but now the smell made her queasier. She had picked at her salad to get something in her, and eating her roll finally settled her stomach enough for her to eat a decent amount of her meal. Dr. Morana watched her intently, as if he were trying to figure something out. She decided to ignore him, preferring instead to talk to Julie about where they bought their gowns. Beck seemed content to gulp at his wine and pick at his chicken.

When the best man rose to give the speech, Nataliya realized that at some point the waiters had put a glass of champagne at her place setting. Everyone else had one too. She must have zoned out while talking to Julie. She felt weirdly out of body for a moment. She was probably just too hot. It did feel kind of warm in the ballroom, probably from all the bodies and the excitement.

"I've known Jose my entire life," the man said. Nataliya couldn't remember his name. "When he told me he found the girl he was going to marry, I thought he was crazy. Not because of Adriana, but because I knew for a fact that Jose had never actually met Salma Hayek."

Beck snorted, and Nataliya was pretty sure that it wasn't because he thought the joke was funny. Since she still hadn't met Jose, Nataliya didn't understand any of the jokes or stories the best man told, so she tuned the speech out and shifted in her seat.

"So, to Jose, my brother in spirit, you chose well. Adriana, welcome to the family. You were everything I wanted for Joey, and I'm so happy you're in our lives." He lifted his glass and spoke in Spanish.

Nataliya raised her glass and moved to take a sip with everyone else when Dr. Morana grabbed her wrist.

"What are you doing?" she hissed.

"You shouldn't be—I mean, you're not supposed to—" he stammered.

Both Julie and Beck stared at him in shock. No one else seemed to notice the commotion. Beck had downed the champagne in one swallow.

"What are you talking about?" Nataliya asked. She took the glass in her other hand and set it on the table. Only then did Dr. Morana let go of her.

"Nothing, never mind." He turned to listen to the maid of honor's speech.

"No seriously, what was that about? That was weird, Dr. Morana."

"You're not pregnant, are you?" Beck asked, his tone almost disinterested. Dr. Morana's face turned paper white.

Nataliya gasped and knocked over the champagne glass as she jumped to her feet. "What the *fuck*?"

CHAPTER NINE

Patrick didn't know who he was more upset by, Nataliya for swearing so loudly at a formal reception, Beck for asking such an impolite question, or himself for losing control and grabbing Nataliya's arm. Regardless, Nataliya had grabbed his arm and dragged him out of the ballroom. No one had said anything as they did so, and Patrick dearly hoped Adriana wouldn't kill him.

Once they were in the hallway by the bathrooms, Nataliya shoved his arm. "What the hell was that, Dr. Morana?"

"I'm not the one who asked."

"No, but you made Beck assume I'm pregnant."

Patrick licked his lips. He didn't know what to say. He knew beyond a shadow of a doubt that she was pregnant. He'd suspected it for a week, but now he knew. After he'd seen the pregnant bridesmaid and gathered a sense for her energy, he could feel it radiating from Nataliya. He could always sense death, but he could also sense life. How on earth could he begin to tell her that? He felt at a loss. He wrung his hands together, wondering how on earth he was going to get himself out of this awful situation. And at his colleague's wedding no less.

"Well," he said finally. "You were sick a lot. And dizzy. I guess I just assumed. Aren't you?"

Nataliya clenched her hands into fists. "I don't know."

"You don't know?" Patrick was shocked. In spite of her trying to drink the champagne, he would have figured she did know and was just waiting to announce it. "But I thought you were angry because I brought it up without your permission." He coughed. "You were the one who made a scene."

Nataliya threw her hands up in the air. "Oh, so now this is all my fault?"

It had definitely been the wrong thing to say. He looked toward the door to the ballroom. No one had come after them, so he hoped the maid of honor was giving her speech. At least Nataliya's outburst had come between the speeches. It would be easy to edit out of the wedding video.

"No! I'm sorry. Nothing is your fault. Look, I'm sorry I even brought it up. If I had concerns, I should have brought them up to you in private. And even then, it's not my business."

Nataliya started pacing, her heels clacking on the floor. "After this reception, you are buying me a pregnancy test."

He couldn't argue with that. Patrick knew he had to be careful about how he handled the situation. He didn't know the circumstances of who she'd been with, though he was pretty sure it was her ex-boyfriend, and he could understand someone in a high-stress fellowship not paying as close attention to their body as they might have otherwise. On top of all that, Nataliya was involved in investigating the bizarre string of murders and it was enough for anyone to be overwhelmed.

"I'm sorry," Patrick said again. "I really didn't mean to make such a mess of everything. I don't want to intrude on your personal life. That has nothing to do with me. But I'll help you in any way I can, all right? If you are pregnant, that doesn't affect the fellowship at all."

He couldn't tell if that had been a worry of hers or not, and she didn't seem comforted by his words. She just shrugged. "Fine, whatever. You can go back in. I'm going to use the bathroom."

"I'll make sure Beck and Julie won't say anything to you."

She didn't seem to care. He watched her go into the ladies' room. He had really screwed up. He went back into the ballroom and saw the maid of honor was still standing and talking. He stayed by the door, not wanting to be intrusive. Once the speech and toast were done, he hurried back to the table.

"Is everything okay?" Julie asked once he sat down. The string quartet had packed up during the speeches, and another band was setting up.

"I hope so," Patrick said, taking a drink of his champagne. "Nataliya will be back soon."

"Is she pregnant?" Beck asked. "Dude, I'm so sorry, I shouldn't have said anything."

"She doesn't know if she is. Don't make a big deal about it, okay? She didn't even realize it was a possibility until you said anything."

"Yikes," Julie said, her eyebrows shooting to her hairline.

"Yeah. So, just act like nothing happened, okay? Adriana is going to ream me out later for causing the scene," Patrick said, taking another sip of champagne.

"All right," Beck agreed. "It's not our business anyway, I guess."

Julie nodded. "Never ask a woman if she's pregnant. Just a good policy all around." She gave a sidelong glance at Beck. "Some people never learned that lesson."

Beck rolled his eyes and took a long swallow of a pale ale he'd appropriated at some point while Patrick was in the hallway.

Jose led Adriana toward the dance floor, and their first dance was announced. The band started playing "Can't Help Falling in Love." The lights dimmed so that there was one light above Adriana and Jose.

"Oh, for the love of god," Beck muttered. "Why did I come to this wedding?"

"Because you wanted the free booze," Julie said, her tone dry.

He glared at her. At that moment, Nataliya pulled out her chair, startling all of them.

No one said anything, but the singer of the band started warbling out the lyrics in a good approximation of Elvis Presley and would have drowned them out anyway.

"The cake better be good," Nataliya said, just loud enough for Patrick to hear. He couldn't help but smirk.

"I know you're probably not happy with me, but I hope you'll still dance with me at least once," he said.

"Of course," she said, managing a smile. "I highly doubt Beck would be a fit partner." She looked over at the detective who was almost finished with his beer. Patrick frowned. Beck had promised he wouldn't get drunk at the wedding. The last time Patrick had tried to bring up Beck's drinking habits, it hadn't gone well. The two men were good friends, and Beck was going through something Patrick couldn't even imagine, but finding comfort in a bottle was not going to fix anything.

"Good," Patrick said finally. "Also, I'm going to have to buy Adriana another gift to make up for this whole thing. I'll add your name too."

"You'd better, Dr. Morana," Nataliya said, and he was pretty sure she was only halfway joking. "But let's pretend it didn't happen, okay? I don't want to ruin the party, and I came here to have fun. Right?"

"Right," Patrick said with a nod. He looked down at his half-drunk glass of champagne. Easier said than done. The guilt he felt over the whole situation wasn't going to go away just because Nataliya was pretending it hadn't happened.

He could tell that Nataliya was having a hard time pretending. When Adriana and Jose made their rounds, Adriana had plastered on a fake smile and given each of them a hug. Nataliya apologized for her outburst, and Adriana waved it away. "You didn't interrupt the speech. I'm just curious as to what Dr. Morana said." She laughed, and Patrick grimaced. He knew that laughter. There was no humor in it. She hugged him, squeezing a little tight. She whispered into his ear, "You are damn lucky that wasn't during the speech, Morana." She let go of him and introduced Jose to Nataliya. Jose was an easy-going guy, and he apparently thought the entire situation hilarious.

"You certainly made it memorable," he said, shaking Nataliya's hand. "Thank you so much for coming."

Nataliya flashed her first genuine smile. Figures that Jose would have pulled it out of her.

"Let's dance," Patrick said to her after the happy couple moved to the next table. Beck left to order another drink, and Julie disappeared.

"Sure." Nataliya took his hand, and he led her to the dance floor. The song was "Can't Take My Eyes Off You" by Frankie Valli, and Patrick felt somewhat embarrassed. He had always thought Nataliya was beautiful, but dressed up, she was stunning. She was happy enough to let him lead and even looked surprised as he led them into actual swing dance steps. Once Nataliya realized he could dance, she relaxed and let herself add some flair to her movements. It was amazing to see her transform from a stressed-and-hiding-it young woman to a passionate dancer.

He was reluctant to leave. When the next song, Glen Miller's "In the Mood" started, Nataliya didn't let go of his hand and pulled him back into more steps. It was a blast. He was impressed by her own moves, especially because she'd worn heels and had been so exhausted in her early stages of pregnancy. From then on it was clear that neither of them wanted to return to their seats. They danced to song after song, from "I Feel Good" by James Brown to "Crazy Little Thing Called Love" to "Come On Eileen."

Finally, the band started playing a slow song. It was Ray LaMontagne, at least he thought so. It was hard to tell when it was sung by another man. Still, Nataliya didn't leave the floor. He pulled her closer, wrapping an arm around her waist and holding her hand in his. She let him, and he felt a sense of relief. He didn't want to overstep.

He had to admit to himself the affection he felt for her was far more than that of a boss for a talented employee. More than that of a mentor and a mentee. He couldn't allow himself to feel that way for her, for many reasons. But he just wanted one moment to enjoy dancing with her. They were both pretending things were different, and while they were in a sumptuous wedding hall with an amazing band, wearing fancy clothes, the fantasy was real even for a few minutes.

When the song was over, Nataliya pulled away from him. "I'm thirsty," she said. She went back to their table, and Patrick drifted toward the bar. When he stepped up to the woman tending the bar, he met her eyes.

A middle-aged woman drives in her car, the rain sheeting down the windshield. She can't see, so she turns the windshield wipers up. They do nothing.

The stream of headlights is broken, a monstrous tree falling onto the road.

"Oh my—"

Her words are cut off when her car slams into the tree.

She doesn't even feel the pain.

"What can I get you, sir?"

The same voice from his vision. He rolled his shoulders back, the ballroom coming back into his awareness. The woman was much younger than in his vision, and his stomach lurched. He needed a drink, but he couldn't have alcohol since he still had to drive. He ordered a soda and a water. He had to drive Nataliya home and pretend that she was just a regular employee he was mentoring. Something about her manner was interesting. While she'd been utterly surprised at her pregnancy, or "possible" pregnancy, she didn't seem angry. Surprised, but not angry. Not upset. Perhaps she wanted to hold off on deeper feelings until she was certain.

He didn't know how she was going to feel about it. Or if she was going to return to her ex. Or if she was even going to tell her ex. It wasn't any of his business, and he had no right to ask her. He desperately wanted to know. He felt protective over Nataliya. There was so much of the world that she didn't know about. That most people didn't know about.

Patrick needed to keep his distance. For her sake. He couldn't reveal who he truly was to anyone. He closed his eyes and took in a deep breath as he waited for his drinks.

Oh, what he would have given to have a normal life.

Nataliya threw the box of condoms at Alex's face. He woke up with a start, a half-strangled yelp escaping his lips. "These are defective, dumbass," she said.

"What?" Alex blinked a few times. "What are you talking about? How did you get into my house?"

"I dated you for two years. You literally showed me where you hid your spare key." Nataliya turned around and left the room. She had thought briefly of waiting until after she'd gone to an OB-GYN, but after taking the pregnancy test when she got home from the wedding the night before, she let her frustration boil over.

"Wait! Talya!" Alex bounded out of his room, only wearing his boxers. "What do you mean the condoms are defective?"

"You're a doctor, you figure it out." Nataliya went into his kitchen and helped herself to his carton of orange juice. He bought the super nice, premium brand. She was still a resident while they dated, and he was making good money as a neurosurgeon. He could afford the high-quality groceries while she couponed.

"Are you pregnant?" he asked, running a hand through his hair.

"Yes."

"And it's mine?" he asked.

Nataliya was at least gratified that he wasn't incredulous when he asked.

"You're the only person I've ever slept with, Alex. It's yours."

He let out a long breath and sat down at his kitchen table. "Oh damn," he said.

"Yeah." She took her glass of juice and sat across from him. "We both always wanted kids. I just didn't think we'd have one after we broke up, you know?"

He managed to give her a half-smile. Alex also knew better than to ask to get back together.

"Did you go to the doctor yet?" he asked.

She shook her head and took a gulp of the juice. "I just found out last night. I wanted to tell you in case you wanted to come with me. I don't know. I don't hate you, Alex. I'm not even mad at you. I know you'll be a good dad."

Alex rubbed his shoulder. "Nataliya, I'll support you in whatever way you need.

"I know you will." She reached across the table and took his hand. "You're gonna be a great dad. I just don't think you were a great boyfriend for me. I know you'd like for us to get married and raise the baby together, but I can't do that. I don't want the same career goals as you. I don't want to have to change myself for you to succeed. But I want you to be in this kid's life. I want this kid to know his or her grandparents on your side, and their cousins. I'm tired and mixed up and scared. It would be so easy to come back to you, to drop the fellowship, to just stop. I don't know."

Alex was clearly confused by her words. "What are you talking about? Why would you drop the fellowship? Your boss didn't ask you, did he?"

"No, no, Dr. Morana's been great. He even realized I was pregnant before I did. But it's hard, you know? And we have this weird string of murders that we can't figure out what the hell happened. And finding out I'm going to have a baby in a few months is daunting. I can't tell my boss any of this stuff. Eva's stressed out enough with work, and so are all of my other friends. Sometimes I feel like you're the only one I can tell stuff to. We've known each other for so long and we were so close."

"I get it," Alex said. He squeezed her hand. "We may not be partners anymore, but we can still be friends, right?"

"Yes. That would be good. Friends. Coparenting." She laughed. "We'll make it work."

"If anyone could make it work," he said, "it would be you. You're far smarter than me, anyway."

She smirked, though she knew he wasn't just being flattering. People who weren't intelligent didn't go to med school when they were nineteen. He always praised her intelligence, even if he felt she wasn't doing enough with it. But no criticisms were forthcoming. He was probably too thrilled at the prospect of being a dad.

"Your mother is going to lose her mind," she said. "She never liked me."

"Mom can suck it up," Alex said with a roll of his eyes. "And she doesn't dislike you. She just thought your career path was gross."

"She does realize that you had to cut on cadavers in med school, right?"

"Yeah, but I'm helping people with brain tumors." He chuckled. "Anyway, my dad loves you, and he's going to love this kid. After all, they had my sister after only being married for three months, so they really don't have a lot of room to talk."

Nataliya nodded. She hadn't really noticed the connection between his mother's attitude and his own before. But it didn't matter anyway. She closed her eyes and finished her juice. She'd make an appointment with a friend she'd met at WashU. The advantage of going to a very well-respected medical school was that she had her pick of doctors for anything. If she didn't know somebody, one of her former classmates would. Alex would go with her. She liked the idea of being friends.

As they talked about plans and appointments, her thoughts drifted to the night before. How had Dr. Morana known? She didn't believe his explanation, not really. Something about the way he acted toward her was off. He'd danced with her all night. It was wonderful, and she loved every moment of it. It was nice to have a normal night, in spite of the revelation that she was pregnant. He'd been so utterly certain she was pregnant, and he hadn't started acting unsure until she called him out on it.

How on earth did her boss, a coroner, figure out she was pregnant? He wasn't a woman. Her mother would have figured it out quickly. He wasn't an obstetrician. He just knew things. Once or twice in the autopsy theater he'd said something about the body and it would turn out to be right. She supposed he was just that good at his job, but now it seemed odd. He rarely let his emotions show, and his steadiness had been a great asset to her during her short time at the morgue.

The way he'd held her when they danced to the Ray LaMontagne song had been intimate. Not necessarily sexual, but they'd definitely been dancing in a way that people of their business relationship shouldn't. She didn't regret it.

Did she have a crush on her boss? Perish the thought. He was always so reserved. Until last night, when he danced and danced well.

Maybe it was just hormones. Hormones explained everything. At least she hoped.

CHAPTER TEN

The papers on Patrick's desk were in perfect order. Julie didn't bother to look in the filing cabinet, as that was a touch too invasive even for her. She flipped through the autopsy reports filled out by Nataliya. Julie wondered how the young woman was doing. After Beck's stunning display of etiquette at the wedding, the girl was probably dealing with a lot. Julie had wanted to stay longer at the reception to talk to her, to make sure that Nataliya would be okay, but she'd gotten a phone call from her boss. Julie left the wedding, a bit irritated at losing more time to enjoy being dressed up and to make sure Beck didn't get too drunk. But duty called, and the FBI didn't wait for anyone.

The door to the office opened and Patrick swept in carrying a travel mug. He stopped short when he saw Julie sitting at his desk.

"What are you doing here?" he asked.

"Denise let me in. That lady is a gem, I tell you." Julie smiled and stood up. She stepped aside so Patrick could sit down.

"That explains how you got here, not why." Patrick shed his coat, scarf, and hat and crossed to sit at his desk. He set down his mug.

Julie sat across from him and crossed her legs. She wore her work clothes. This was not a social visit. "We have four confirmed victims in the area," she said. She didn't need to expand on which victims.

"Four?

"Yes. Two nights ago, Adriana's wedding. The body was discovered outside of the state, which is why you weren't informed."

"Where?" Patrick asked, putting his travel mug down. He looked quite perplexed.

"Illinois again. Pere Marquette State Park."

"That's almost an hour north of here." Patrick shook his head.

"Yes. Whoever is doing this is heading north. I have requested that the autopsy information be sent here for your review."

"I never really asked you why you wanted me to review the cases outside of my jurisdiction," Patrick said. He took a sip from his mug. "I only wanted to see the Alton case for my own curiosity, but you've been pushing it, getting the local departments to give me the case files. Why?"

"You're good at what you do," Julie said. She shrugged, though she knew she couldn't play coy for very long. Patrick was good at other things as well.

"Do you think it's a serial killer? Not just a serial rapist?"

"I wouldn't have you review the case files if I didn't."

Patrick chuckled. "Why aren't you having your FBI medical examiners do this? I work for the county here, not for the FBI."

"We've been known to look outside the bureau for consultation," she answered with a smile.

Patrick just stared at her. She had a good poker face, but dammit, Patrick could be downright spooky when he wanted to be. Like he knew something she didn't know. Which was true. And why she was in his office.

"How's Nataliya doing?" Julie asked.

If the sudden subject change threw him, he certainly didn't show it. "I haven't spoken to her since I drove her home after the wedding reception." He said it so conversationally. He'd be a good FBI agent if he ever wanted to be.

"Is she coming in soon?"

"I gave her the day off," Patrick replied. "She hasn't had one since she started here, and she's exhausted. These murders are bothering her more than she's letting on."

"Really? I mean, I understand being upset at the one we found in Forest Park, but I'm sure she saw worse in school."

"No, not like that. Dr. Vasilyeva is incredibly intelligent. She probably could have graduated from high school even earlier than she did, based on what little she's told me about her education. She's adept at figuring out causes of death, and her diagnostic mind is remarkable. She's upset because she can't figure out how these victims died. How their hearts collapsed like they did."

Julie thought for a moment, tapping her fingers on the arm of the chair. "You could just tell her," she said.

Patrick reacted. It wasn't much, just a little jerk of the head. She smiled, amused that she'd finally thrown him off his guard. "What are you talking about?" he asked.

"Their hearts weren't collapsed by any natural method, Dr. Morana. You know that as well as I do. They didn't have heart defects or heart attacks, and nothing they ate did this to them." She knew that playing chicken with him wasn't the most mature thing to do, but she wanted to see how long it was before he'd break.

He looked at her, his brows furrowed. "Of course, nothing they ate did this to them. That's a weird thing to say."

"No, it's not," she said.

"If you have something you want to ask, just ask, Agent Lyons. I have a full day today, and I'm not in the mood for petty games."

She nearly chuckled. He wasn't playing. She'd gotten a good sense of him in their interactions since she came to St. Louis, and she knew he played things very close to the vest. It was more than just professional privacy. He was hiding something, and she might not have realized it if she were, say, someone like Detective Beck. Or even Nataliya.

"Fine, Dr. Morana. I'll be straight with you. I had a feeling you were the type who wouldn't give an inch." At his confused look, she continued, "I'm having you investigate these deaths because most medical examiners, even with the FBI, wouldn't know where to start. You do, because you've seen stranger things." Julie frowned. "These women were murdered, and it was by supernatural means. Most likely black magic."

Patrick didn't react. He stared at her with that same, reserved, calculating look. She couldn't imagine what he was thinking. So, she continued speaking. "The stomach contents of these girls were unusual, especially since they didn't have much else besides these herbs. I looked them up, and I can't find anything that means it was part of a real 'spell' for lack of a better word. I had hoped you might have more insight."

Patrick gave a slow blink. "Why would you assume that?" he asked. This time his tone wasn't one of confusion. He was curious.

"Because I know things. Sometimes," Julie said, not bothering to clarify her meaning.

"Because of the FBI?"

She shook her head. "In fact, I'm only in St. Louis because I pulled a nice Fox Mulder move," she said with a chuckle. "I got sent here as punishment. I was working my way pretty high up. High aspirations. Then I stumbled onto a few things I couldn't explain, and I really tried. My honesty wasn't well appreciated by the bureau. But they couldn't fire me, so they sent me here. Just my luck, I get to work with you."

"Very lucky," Patrick said. He smiled. "I must say that this does present an opportunity. I have quite an array of books in my possession. The stomach contents of the victims align perfectly with a love potion. A fake potion, by the way. The book I found it in was marketed as a historical look at amusing primitive beliefs. Some people took it as real."

"A fake love potion?" Julie thought for a moment. "I guess the rapist tried to drug them first, and when it didn't work, he just raped them?"

Patrick shrugged. "I don't know anything about that. I'm not entirely sure the rapist and the murderer are the same person. Someone stupid enough to use a fake love potion wouldn't have the ability to squeeze a person's heart until it collapses without leaving a single mark elsewhere on the body."

She hadn't really considered that before, but it was worth looking into. The lack of evidence on the bodies or at the crime scene was particularly frustrating for forensics. "All right then. Could they be connected? I mean they have to be, right?"

"I don't know. I told you I'm not a homicide detective. I don't know the motive. I wouldn't even know how to question a suspect. I just look at the evidence and give my professional opinion."

"Look, Dr. Morana, I'm not asking in an official capacity. I can't ask in an official capacity because then I'd really be fired for investigating something that officially doesn't exist. I don't know much about this area. I grew up in Washington DC, and then I worked in New York for the past few years. I just want to know where to start looking."

"I understand," Patrick said, this time with more compassion. "There is a voodoo community in this area. Much larger than you'd ever expect. They keep it very quiet, though sometimes you can see evidence if you know how to look. I don't recommend trying to speak to any of them. They wouldn't talk to me, and they really wouldn't talk to a fed."

"You think someone did this with voodoo?"

"Not in the slightest. This isn't what they do. They keep a close eye on what happens in the area. Voodoo practitioners can't afford to let people think that what they do is evil, murderous, black magic. I bring them up because I'm sure someone in that religion will probably know something."

Julie nodded. She knew enough about Louisiana Voodoo to know that the religion wasn't what most media portrayed it as. And she didn't blame them for their secrecy. "If they won't talk to either one of us, how do we find out if they know anything?"

Patrick let out a sigh. "That's the difficult part. I do have a contact, who can contact them. It's unfortunately going to be a game of telephone, but it's all we have."

"Fine. Once you get the case file on the fourth victim, try and see if you can get any information." Julie stood up. "I'm running blind here. Whoever is raping and murdering these women isn't going to stop."

"I agree," Patrick said with a nod. "And the more people that we make aware of what's going on, the more likely we are to make this person stop. I'll try my best working with my contact. If things go well, I'll pass along your name. Since you're aware, my contact will probably want to speak with you."

"Probably?"

He shrugged. "It's not every day you find someone who works for the federal government who actually admits the shitty stuff they know."

"I don't know if aliens exist, I don't know who shot Martin Luther King Jr., and there is no smoking man at the FBI headquarters. At least since they banned smoking indoors."

Patrick blinked. "What?"

"The X-files," Julie said with a chuckle. "Dana Scully was my inspiration, you know. To join the FBI. I'll talk to you later. I have to get to the office. Let Nataliya know I hope she feels better soon, and that she should call me if she needs anything. There are some things that you just can't talk to a man about, you know?' She winked. Patrick didn't so much as roll his eyes. He really was a tough nut to crack. She left, feeling a tiny bit better about the trajectory of the case. Only a tiny bit, but at least it was something.

"*Privyet*, Mama!" Nataliya gave a fake smile to Denise, who was eating her lunch at the table in the break room. For once Nataliya was glad that she spoke to her parents in Russian on the phone. Her mother, with her uncanny sense of Nataliya's moods, immediately sighed.

"What's wrong, Natasha?" her mother asked.

"I'm not coming home for Christmas," Nataliya said. There was no use beating around the bush. Her mother was direct to a fault.

Denise looked slightly disappointed that Nataliya was speaking in Russian. She probably wanted to eavesdrop. The old lady was sweet, but she had her faults.

"Why not?"

"This fellowship has been a lot of work. And there's a suspected serial rapist and murderer around here. I'd feel weird leaving and going so far away."

"We never see you as it is, Natashenka."

Nataliya bit her lip. Her mother only called her that pet name when Nataliya was upset about something. Or her mother was upset about something. "*Prosti*, but you knew when I left for college that I wasn't going to be able to see you as much."

"*Da*, but that was not our choice. That was yours." Her mother sighed again. "Papa is going to be sad."

"I know. I miss you two very much. Christmas in St. Louis isn't the same as Christmas in Minnesota."

"Maybe we should come visit you?"

Nataliya felt a flare of panic. Christmas was only a week away, and she had not decided when to tell her parents about her pregnancy. Her doctor's appointment with Alex had gone well, but she was still freaked out by the whole situation. "No, no, I'm sure plane tickets would be expensive. And Eva and I haven't been keeping up with the apartment well. It's a busy time of year for her, and I'm always at the morgue. One of the other examiners just got married and she's away, so I have more work to do. I'm sorry, but I'm so tied up."

"You don't want to see us? We can stay in a hotel, Nataliya. We'd spend any amount of money to see you. We're not paupers."

"*Prosti! Prosti!* I didn't mean it like that, Mama. I just don't want to put you two out."

"You don't want to see your poor mother. I understand. Well, call us on Christmas Eve so that I know you're not killing yourself working. *Vse, poka.*"

Her mother disconnected after her farewell. She looked at her phone. That had not gone well. She wondered if the Russian mothers in her community had regular meetings on how to guilt their grown children. Once Nataliya revealed her pregnancy, nothing on the earth would stop Sofia Vasilyeva from flying out to St. Louis to baby her. Being an only child was rough sometimes, especially the child of parents who lived through the dying days of the Soviet era and escaped the uncertain times after its fall.

Nataliya left the break room and went into her office. Patrick was gone for the day, testifying in a court case. It seemed a bit late in the year for a criminal case, but he'd told her the trial was dragging on. Thankfully Patrick only had to be there for one day. She was alone in the morgue that day, as Dr. Hammond had already left and Dr. Paulson was on her honeymoon until after Christmas.

Things had quieted down at the morgue. She supposed that they'd get some winter-frozen corpses before too long, but there had been fewer violent deaths. It was a nice break, especially after the wedding and her pregnancy preparations. She didn't have much time to speak to Patrick outside of work-related musings, and she'd begged off going out to the pub on the weekends. It felt weird only ordering water. She didn't need alcohol to enjoy herself, but it felt like that was the whole point for the other three to go out. To unwind after a long week of crime and death.

Someone knocked on the open door of the office. She looked up to see Beck standing there. "Hey there," she said, putting aside her book on forensic anthropology. She'd been studying during her little downtime. "To what do I owe the pleasure?"

Beck chuckled. "I came to see Patrick, actually."

"He's in court today. Can I help you with anything?"

"Nah, not really. I just wanted to see if he could knock off early and get a drink. It's not the weekend, but, well, sometimes you just need to take a break, you know?"

"Certainly." Nataliya smiled. "I'd offer to go with you, but as you so adroitly pointed out at the wedding, alcohol is *zapreshenee*."

At his confused look, she chuckled. "It means 'prohibited' in Russian."

"You speak Russian, then?"

"Yes, I was born in Russia. I became a naturalized citizen as a young teenager."

Beck thought about that for a moment, but when he spoke, it was clear he'd been thinking of something else. "Since I'm here, I should apologize to you. Asking if you were pregnant, that was pretty damn rude. I'm really sorry." He took a couple of steps into the office and leaned against Patrick's desk.

"You're forgiven, Beck. I'm more embarrassed about the whole situation more than anything else. I had no idea at all. And I didn't even understand what Dr. Morana was doing until you said anything. I can't blame you for speaking your mind, especially since you'd had a couple drinks."

Beck rubbed his forehead. "Yeah, that was not my finest moment, though. I knew better than to drink too much, but I didn't realize how hard it would be to attend a wedding so soon after everything in my life fell apart. I'm sure Patrick told you that my private life is in shambles."

"He didn't give me many details." Nataliya shrugged. "I'm sorry that you're dealing with a divorce. I can't imagine how difficult that would be. My parents moved here when I was a baby and they barely spoke English, but they stuck it out and got closer. I'm lucky that I have their example."

"Yeah, my parents stayed together until my dad died." He shook his head. "It's hard to want to stay with someone who cheated on you twice because you weren't what the other person truly wanted." He let out a sigh. "I'm sorry, I'm sure you don't care about any of this."

"I don't mind," Nataliya said. "Sometimes it's nice to just get it all out."

"I should have kicked her out the first time, but, well, I didn't want to believe it." He let out a mirthless laugh. "Anyway, maybe I should hold off on drinking tonight. Patrick is usually who I go to when things get bad. And it's bad with the lawyers. I'm not the one who threw the marriage in the garbage. Julie's super busy this week too, trying to get everything finished up as well as she can before the holidays. She's going home to visit her folks, so she won't be around for a week or so."

"Are you doing anything for Christmas?" Nataliya asked.

"Most of my family lives in the area, so we'll probably go to my older brother's farm." Beck shrugged. "It's what we usually do. I'm not looking forward to all the questions about my ex."

"What does Dr. Morana usually do? Is he a gift type of guy? I've been trying to find little things for everyone here."

Beck gave her a funny look, and she felt taken aback. "You didn't ask him, did you?"

"Ask him what he does for Christmas?" Nataliya furrowed her brow.

"Yeah."

"No, it never came up."

Beck nodded. "Don't. He's really weird about his family. I've known him for a few years now, and he gets real squirrelly if you ask him anything about it. I don't know if he celebrates Christmas or not, but he usually attends Denise's Christmas Eve party."

"Oh, I'd completely forgotten about that." Nataliya looked at her desk calendar. She hadn't marked it down, though the invitation was in her top desk drawer. "Thanks for the tip. I wouldn't want to offend him. Dr. Morana has been really great to me, and I really want to keep up the good relationship."

"So, question."

She looked back up at him, a bit perplexed. He had such an odd way of speaking for a man in his thirties. It was like he had the vernacular of a teenager sometimes. "What?"

"Why do you still call him Dr. Morana? He calls you Nataliya most of the time."

She felt a flush rise to her face. "I just want to show him the proper respect. He's my mentor. He's never said anything about it."

"I doubt he ever would." Beck absently picked at his lip with his fingernails. "He can be overly cautious sometimes."

"What do you mean?"

Beck dropped his hand. "I mean, you do realize the guy is absolutely crazy about you, right?"

Nataliya felt her eyes widen. "I'm sorry, what?"

"You seriously haven't noticed it? Hell, how could you not when he was dancing with you at the wedding? My dude couldn't stop looking at you all night. Even after my wondrous blunder, he was completely moonstruck. God, I really thought you noticed."

"Dr. Morana cannot be crazy about me," Nataliya said. "He's my boss, and he's just been so kind to me. I mean, I'm pregnant, barely twenty-six, and I threw up at that crime scene that one time."

Beck chuckled. "Sure, sure, keep believing that. I've known him longer than you, and I can tell when his quiet reservation changes, and something about you definitely caught his attention. Maybe he has a thing for natural redheads, and I just haven't seen him with one before, but I'm pretty sure it's more than that."

Nataliya didn't know how to process this information. Her boss was interested in her? She liked him more than well enough, and she'd had some flashes of affection and desire for him, but he was so impenetrable sometimes. She barely knew him.

"He can't be in love with me," she mumbled to herself in Russian.

"Huh?"

"Nothing, never mind. I'd better finish up here," she said. She wanted to grill Beck for more information on Patrick, but she was also keenly aware that discussing his feelings in his own office while he was gone was odd. "I hope things get better for you, Beck. I'll see you later?"

"Sure." Beck smirked. "Don't act too weird around him now. I doubt he even realizes as much as I do."

"Great, you dump this revelation about his feelings on me, and you don't even know if he knows?"

"I have never been accused of being a wise man. See ya."

Nataliya watched him go, wondering when her life changed from a murder mystery to a romantic drama with a hidden message on the dangers of unprotected sex. Except that whole part where it was protected. She dropped her head on her desk. She was not going to get any studying done now.

CHAPTER ELEVEN

Patrick climbed out of his car, grumbling at how far away he had to park from Denise's house in St. Charles. She lived close to the downtown area, and it was crawling with people enjoying Christmas Traditions, the festival that ran through December. Christmas Eve was the worst. He couldn't find a good parking spot to save his life, and it was freezing cold. No snow, of course. He couldn't remember the last time St. Louis had a white Christmas.

He pulled his scarf up to his ears, cursing that he'd forgotten his hat, and trudged on to Denise's house, four blocks away.

"Dr. Morana! Dr. Morana!"

He looked over his shoulder. In the twilight, he saw Nataliya rushing towards him. "No need to run!" he called out. "I don't want you to slip!"

She slowed up, conscious of the ice on the sidewalks. She was bundled up much better than he was, with a handknit scarf and hat that matched, and fine leather gloves. Her long wool coat had fur on the collar, and he could tell it was real. Dead animals weren't the easiest to sense, but something about fur always sent him tingling. "That's an interesting coat," he said, looking it up and down.

"My mom brought it from Russia," she replied. "St. Louis has nothing on Petrozavodsk."

"I have never heard of it, but I don't doubt it." He managed a smile. Things had been somewhat strained between them for the past week, and he wasn't sure why. She didn't really converse with him much outside of their work, less than usual anyway, and she seemed to avoid him whenever she could. He had assumed it was because of her pregnancy, but he didn't want to say anything.

"I've never been here on the holidays," she said, gesturing toward the lights downtown. "I've always been so busy with finals or leaving to spend time with my parents once I had a break."

"It's fun, if you're into that sort of thing. Victorian Santa, Christmas carols, lots of little shops." He shrugged. It wasn't particularly his sort of thing, but he'd never had much cause to celebrate since he was a teenager. He shivered at a memory that crawled into his head, of Reuel and Henry and a wood-burning furnace.

"My mom would like it, then," she said with a smile. "I hope Denise's party doesn't go too late, I'm exhausted already."

"You can leave anytime you want," Patrick assured her. "She won't take offense."

She nodded and followed him as he led the way down the sidewalk. Strangely, there wasn't anyone else on the street that he could see. It was getting darker, and the streetlights hadn't come on yet. He stopped short. Something caught his attention. Something very, very wrong.

"What's the matter?" Nataliya asked, nearly bumping into him. She touched his arm, and he whipped his hand up to shush her. He looked ahead, scowling as he squinted.

"Do you see that?" he asked, pointing into the alley.

"No."

"Shh." He took her hand and crept closer to the alley between the buildings. They were in a commercial area, and both buildings seemed abandoned. He could see two figures in the darkness. Then, he heard a voice.

"Come on, you stupid slut. You're supposed to want this."

"Oh my—"

Patrick slapped his hand over Nataliya's mouth, cutting off her exclamation. She struggled against him, and he held her tighter as he pulled her away. "Call 911." He let go of her and dashed into the alley where a man was struggling with a young woman's clothes. She gasped for breath but didn't scream, and she fought hard against the man.

"Get away from her!" Patrick raced forward and moved to grab the man, but he stopped short as three sets of eyes turned toward him. Three. The girl, the man, and the thing riding the man's shoulders.

His breath caught in his throat. No. Not possible. Such things didn't happen anymore.

"Get the fuck out of here," the man said, slashing at Patrick with a knife.

Patrick dodged the knife and grabbed the man's arm. He twisted it so that the man was on his knees in the refuse of the alley, screaming in pain as Patrick popped his shoulder out of its socket. He pushed even more and the man's arm snapped.

As if ungagged, the girl let out an earsplitting scream. That was enough to bring over Nataliya who had her cell phone to her ear. She stopped mid word as she stared at the man. The thing on his shoulders jumped off and flew at Patrick's face. It was hard to see its form, even accounting for the dim alley. Patrick threw his hands up to cover himself, and the thing bounced off with a wild shriek of pain. It flew upwards into the cloudy sky, screaming *"SON OF DEATH! SON OF DEATH!"* in the Dead Tongue. Patrick sank to his knees, the agony in his forearms excruciating. The thing's claws had melted through his coat sleeves, straight to his skin. He didn't know if he was bleeding or burnt.

"Quick, send an ambulance," Nataliya said. "It looks as if the rapist has a broken arm, and my friend is bleeding. Okay. Yes, I'll stay on. Patrick, are you okay?"

Patrick looked at his arms, blinking wildly. "Huh?" He turned his gaze to her. Her pale face peeked out from underneath her knit hat.

"The police should be here any minute," she said. She dropped her phone and ran to the girl. "Are you okay? Are you hurt?" She began checking the girl, who had stopped screaming.

"I don't know," the girl said. She started rubbing her chest. She wore no coat, and her shirt had been unbuttoned all the way. It looked as if the man was in the process of cutting her bra when he was interrupted. The man lay on the ground, moaning.

"Did he do anything to you?" Nataliya asked. She pulled off her coat and wrapped it around the girl.

"No. At least I don't think so." The girl rubbed her mouth. "He made me eat this weird stuff. I couldn't say anything. It felt like my heart was going to burst. Did I have a heart attack?"

Patrick moved closer, but he couldn't seem to form a coherent sentence.

"I don't think so, but we should get you checked out. We're both doctors." Wisely, she said nothing about their specialty. She began systematically checking the girl over, making sure she wasn't injured in places they couldn't see. As she was checking her over, the police and the ambulance arrived at the same time.

Nataliya quickly pointed out the rapist, and told them that Patrick had been the rescuer. Someone started tending to his arms, and he tried to blink away his confusion. Everything was red lights, green lights, blue lights. Christmas lights. Police lights. The monster that had attacked him was powerful, and he hadn't prepared for it. He had no idea that he was going to be attacked by a rabisu.

"Dr. Morana? Dr. Morana?" He couldn't feel his head in order to turn it. "Patrick! Look at me!"

Nataliya had never used his name before. Well, she'd tried once. He turned to look at her and he shook his head to clear it. "Natashenka" he said, pushing away the paramedic who was checking his pulse. He pulled Nataliya into his arms. He could feel her shivering from the cold. "Where'd your coat go?" he asked, and then immediately remembered she'd given it to the girl. "You should have stayed back."

"I couldn't leave you alone, Patrick. You need to let go of me so they can finish looking you over."

He didn't let go though. He closed his eyes, breathed in the smell of her. Her hair and the wool of her scarf. He didn't want to forget that smell, no matter what happened. Woodsmoke still conjured the worst memories of his life. That last Christmas as a teenager. "I can't let you do that again," he whispered. "It'd destroy me if I got you hurt."

She didn't say anything, and for that he was glad. He felt the paramedics pull him away from her, and he couldn't tear his eyes away from her concerned face as they helped him into the ambulance. "I need to call Denise," she said, "and we need to talk to the police. I'll drive separately, okay?"

He nodded, not daring to argue. She seemed overwhelmed by his reaction, or maybe it was the scene they had witnessed. He couldn't pull himself together. Patrick knew it would take a while to get his bearings, and it was best if she stayed away from him until he could do so. He didn't want her to pull away from him. Or maybe he should let her. She'd be safer. He never should have danced with her. That was the end, he knew. Dancing. He closed his eyes as the paramedics stripped off his coat and shirt. Dancing with the red-haired girl in a black dress that sparkled like the stars.

Nataliya let out a deep breath. The police had just finished questioning her in the waiting room of the hospital. She desperately wanted to know how Patrick was. And the girl was going to be just fine, at least physically. Patrick had stopped her rapist before he could do anything, and though her heart had some arrhythmia and weakening, it would heal up after a minor surgery. Nataliya clenched her fists. The girl had given her back the coat, thanking her for her generosity. Nataliya had put it to the side, as the waiting room seemed particularly hot. What she'd seen in that alley defied all explanation.

She put a hand on her stomach, wondering if the little life inside could feel her confusion and distress. Before she could contemplate too much longer, Patrick came into the waiting room. He wasn't wearing his coat, and he was only in his undershirt. He looked exhausted.

"Are you all right?" she asked, jumping to her feet and hurrying over.

"I'm fine," he said, though she wasn't sure. She took his arm and turned it so she could look at one of the wounds. It looked like a rug burn, though many times worse. The very edges of the wound were blistered.

"What in the hell? Are they discharging you?" she asked.

"Yep. Not much they can do. They gave me a prescription for the pain and some ointment, but other than that?" He shrugged. "Thank you for waiting, Nataliya."

"Of course. I didn't want you to be stranded here without a car. Did the police talk to you?"

He nodded. He seemed a bit distant, and in a different way than usual. It wasn't out of reservation, but because his mind was on something else.

"Then let's get out of here. Do you feel up to driving? I can take you back to your car."

He looked at his arms and shook his head. "I don't know. They did give me some pain meds, so it's probably not wise for me to drive."

Well, that explained it. He was a bit loopy. She led him out of the waiting room and toward the parking lot. Once he was settled in his seat, she started off. "I'll take you home, okay?"

He nodded somewhat absently. "I'd better get you the directions." He opened the maps app on his phone and turned on the voice commands. He was very quiet as she drove, and she felt like turning on music would be too distracting. It was a bit of a longer drive than she'd expected, as he lived in the Shaw neighborhood. However, most people seemed to be staying in on Christmas Eve, so she didn't have much traffic. Shaw was a beautiful neighborhood, and she was happy to see that he lived in a beautiful brick townhouse. He wasn't too far from the Botanical Gardens either, and she imagined he was the type of person to have a membership so that he could read or walk about in peace when he had a day off. At least, that's what she would do. Being so entrenched in death, enjoying living things was tantamount.

"Thanks for the ride, Nataliya," he said. He hadn't put on his coat in spite of the cold, so that his arms wouldn't be scraped by the fabric.

"Of course, Dr. Morana. Do you need anything? I can run to the store before it closes."

He shook his head. "No, thanks. Well, maybe. I could use something to eat. We didn't get any of Denise's gingerbread." He let out a half-sigh, half-chuckle. He pulled his wallet out of his coat pocket and handed her a couple of twenties. "Here. If you could please get me something to eat, I'd appreciate it. Anything is fine. I guess you know what I like enough. Get yourself something to eat too. Gotta feed her too."

"Her?"

He shrugged. "The baby."

"And you think it's gonna be a girl?" she teased.

"Yes." He exited the car and walked up the steps to his front door. He really was out of it. She'd only meant to be silly, but he took her so seriously. She made sure he was able to unlock his door before she drove off to get something to eat. Nataliya knew he would scold her if she grabbed fast food, more out of concern for her nutrition than his own. Getting an idea, she called in an order and frowned as she realized most of the grocery stores would be closed. She knew at least a couple of pharmacies would be open, so she picked up a few things before the food was ready. When she got back to Patrick's house, she let herself in, as he'd texted her to do just that.

His house was dark, but warm. She moved through the hallway to a room with a light on. Patrick sat on a comfortable chair in what looked to be an office or a library. He'd put on a loose shirt. A book was on the table in front of him, along with several jars of dried herbs and flowers. A photograph had been tucked in between the pages as a bookmark. A mortar and pestle sat on the table as well, and it looked as if he used it. He blinked a few times before acknowledging Nataliya. "You're back," he said. "That smells delicious." He stood up and nearly took one of the bags she held before he stopped short. Without another word he led her into the kitchen. He turned on the lights to reveal a beautiful antique table with cushioned chairs. They had embroidered seats, and she wondered what the pieces were worth. The kitchen also had gorgeous cherry-wood cabinets and black granite countertops. She put the bags on the table. "I called in an order at Georgie's," she said. "They were pretty busy, but I went to school with the owner's son. He swears I helped him pass his third year of medical school by tutoring him in my spare time, so I guess they think they owe me a favor."

"I love Georgie's," Patrick said. He pulled several containers out of the bag, revealing an incredibly appetizing Christmas Eve dinner. She'd ordered glazed ham, mashed potatoes, stuffing, green beans, cranberry sauce, and mincemeat pies. "Wow, you spent a lot more than what I gave you."

"I wanted to make up for missing Denise's party. No, stop," she said as he moved to grab his wallet on the counter. "My Christmas gift to you, Dr. Morana. You've been so good to me, and I wanted to show some of my appreciation. Please, sit down and we'll eat."

"Looks like they sent some eggnog too," Patrick said with a grin.

"Yep. I told them to give me nonalcoholic, since I'm pregnant and your meds shouldn't be mixed."

Patrick smiled down at the feast, looking relieved. It was just food, but for some reason her heart felt full that he was so pleased. All the weirdness that had happened could wait. She wanted to make sure he was truly fine before badgering him. He went to fetch plates and silverware, and Nataliya jumped over to grab them. "I don't want you to use your arms too much yet," she said.

"I'm fine," he said. "You're the pregnant one."

"I don't have blistered wounds on my forearms. Babies can handle a little jostle every now and then. We both took the same medical school classes."

Instead of arguing, he sat down at the table and waited for her to set the plate and silverware in front of them. "You didn't need to go to so much trouble, but thank you. I don't have much occasion to celebrate, except for Denise's parties, and I admit I was disappointed at missing it. I wouldn't trade it, though. Finding the man that's been hurting women is better than anything.

Nataliya watched as he served himself. "What a coincidence that we found him," she murmured.

Patrick stopped for a moment and gave her a long look. He didn't answer her, though, just finished serving himself. She helped herself as well, and the two began eating. "It's times like this that I miss my parents," Nataliya said. "Having them visit would have been too much trouble, but they're my family. It's hard being away from them on holidays."

"You're lucky," Patrick said.

"I suppose I am." She smiled and felt a bit of anxiety when she remembered that Beck had told her not to bring up his family. "My roommate is working all night and spending the day tomorrow with her family in Fenton. So it's just me. I was looking forward to a nice day of reading and hot chocolate and researching baby necessities. I think Alex was going to drop by, but he'll probably be monopolized by his parents. It's the first Christmas I'm going to be alone."

"You don't have to be," Patrick said then. "I don't have any traditions. But if you want, you can—" He coughed. "You can spend it with me."

Beck's other words echoed in her head. She took a bite of ham and thought for a moment. She was tempted, but she couldn't get the thought of what she'd seen out of her head. "Patrick, why did you call me Natashenka? How did you even know that name?"

"When I found out that you were Russian, I did some light research. I wanted to know a bit more about your culture. I was also curious about your name, so I looked it up to see how it was written in Cyrillic. And of course I saw how fond the Russians are of pet names and nicknames. I saw Natashenka. And it suits you, you know." His smile was soft. She wondered if it was the pain meds, the good food, or the romance of the season, but she was dead certain that Beck was right about Patrick's feelings. In spite of the strange thing that attacked him in the alley, it didn't frighten her. Quite the opposite. "Does that bother you?" he asked. "I know that it's not really professional."

"I was just surprised, that's all. I don't mind if you call me that. I would like to call you Patrick, if I can."

He nodded, meeting her gaze with a serious expression.

"Patrick, what happened? In the alley? That wasn't a crow, or a bat, and any bird large enough to look like that wouldn't have been black, I don't think, unless it was a vulture. It also spoke. Like a different language or something."

Patrick lowered his fork and stared down at his plate. "It's called a rabisu. I didn't think there were any left. Clearly, I was wrong."

"What's a rabisu? I've never heard of it."

"It's a demonic creature in the Akkadian mythology."

"Akkadian? Like, the ancient Mesopotamian empire?" Nataliya was surprised that she remembered that bit of ancient history from her undergrad days.

"Yes."

"A demonic creature? Are you kidding me?"

"I wouldn't ever joke about this, Nataliya. In the myths, they crouch in corners, waiting to attack people. I've heard stories about them latching on to people with a vampiric-like draw. Once it realized its host, the rapist, was incapacitated, it attacked me. And when it realized who I truly was, it ran away. Even rabisu fear those who can walk the paths of the dead."

"Did they give you opioids?" Nataliya straightened up in her chair as she studied him.

"I haven't taken anything since I left the hospital." Patrick had stopped eating entirely. "I can't explain it to you. You wouldn't believe me if I told you. You're not even believing what you saw, not that I can blame you. It was dark and we'd just stumbled upon an attempted rape." He pushed up his sleeves, revealing his arms. The burns looked half healed. She stared in shock. She'd worked with burn victims. She knew they didn't look like that with some ointment and an hour and a half of time.

"How?" She couldn't say anything else.

"I heal fast," he said. "Very fast."

"How?"

"Because of who I am." He picked up his fork and ate some mashed potatoes. After a moment, he continued, "And what I know how to do."

Nataliya reached across the table and grabbed the wrist of his free hand. She leaned over to inspect the wounds. She ran her fingers over the healing skin, making sure her movements were gentle. Patrick shivered. "How is this possible?" She looked up into his green eyes. She'd always thought they were beautiful, but now, there was something else in them. A sadness. A resignation. His gaze made her wonder why he had invited her to spend the day with him tomorrow, beyond general affection.

"Because my father is Death."

"I'm sorry, what?" She didn't let go of his wrist. "You have a good sense of humor about your job sometimes, but that's just weird."

"My father is Death. Thanatos. Pale horse. 'And when he had opened the fourth seal, I heard the voice of the fourth beast say, Come and see. And I looked, and behold a pale horse: and his name that sat on him was Death, and Hell followed with him. And power was given unto them over the fourth part of the earth, to kill with sword, and with hunger, and with death, and with the beasts of the earth.' Book of Revelation, Chapter Six, verses seven to eight. King James Bible."

He had recited the verses with the dispassion of someone who'd had to memorize Bible passages for Sunday school every week. There was no hint that he was pulling her leg or even all that serious about the words he'd said. He said them as plainly as if she'd said her parents were from a city in Northern Russia. He continued eating as if he hadn't said the most bizarre thing she'd ever heard.

She looked down at her own plate, not knowing what to say. Her boss didn't seem delusional. And the thing in the alley was strange. And he'd healed fast. Her mind didn't want to process everything. So she didn't.

CHAPTER TWELVE

She hadn't called him insane. Besides her question about opioids, she'd been remarkably calm about the whole thing. Their conversation had faded away and they ate in silence, but it wasn't awkward. It felt relaxing. Once they finished, she handed him a plastic shopping bag.

"What's this?" he asked.

"A present," she said.

He looked inside, a bit confused. "Gingerbread bubble bath, a bottle of Jack Daniel's, and a box of candy canes." He glanced at her, trying not to burst into laughter. "Well, thank you for thinking of me."

"The pharmacy didn't have much," Nataliya said with a giggle. "The Jack Daniel's is your real present. You can't drink it until you're off your pain medications, though. Should I have gotten you the stuffed reindeer instead?"

Patrick shook his head with a chuckle. He pulled out a candy cane and started to unwrap it. "Thank you, Nataliya. It's perfect."

"I was going to get you something else before now, but I couldn't figure out what that should be." she shrugged. "I don't know much about your hobbies or interests."

"I like candy," he said, sticking the end of the cane in his mouth. His tongue ran over a piece of plastic wrap, so he made a face, pulled out the candy cane, and peeled it off. He exchanged an amused glance with Nataliya. He looked at his watch. "It's only eight thirty. It feels much later."

"Yeah. I used to stay up as late as I could, waiting for Santa Claus. And then on New Year's Eve, I'd stay up as late as I could, waiting for Ded Moroz and Snegurochka. That's Grandfather Christmas and the Snowmaiden. We got to celebrate Christmas again on January 7th, since that's the Orthodox Christmas. That's a lot of celebrating for a little girl. But I always loved it. We'd watch American movies, some Russian movies my grandparents sent to us, and make hot chocolate and sit by the fireplace and talk about how different winters were. My parents told me how they never celebrated Christmas, because it was banned in the Soviet Union, and how happy they were that I could celebrate whatever holiday I wanted. When I got older, it made more sense as to why we celebrated so much. They didn't have much growing up, and they didn't have the freedom they do here." Nataliya sighed. "I'm sorry, I'm talking too much."

"I like hearing you talk. It sounds like you had a happy childhood," Patrick said. He liked to imagine her celebrating a cozy holiday as a little red-haired girl.

She smiled at him. "It was. When I was younger, I was so eager to grow up and be a doctor. Now, sometimes I wish I could go back to those days when I didn't have anything more pressing to worry about than some homework and a few chores." She let out a sigh. "I guess we can't go back."

Patrick couldn't really relate. He wouldn't go back to his childhood for anything. "Nataliya, I was telling the truth."

Her animated expression seemed to fade away. "I don't know what to believe, Patrick. The Book of Revelation is an allegory, isn't it? How can Death be a personified figure? It's just death."

"How could I heal so quickly?" He bit a piece off the candy cane and crunched it with his teeth. "I don't know how else to make you believe me. But you're not afraid of me."

"No, of course not. You helped that girl in the alley. And you didn't treat me any differently once you found out I was pregnant. And you knew the circumstances."

He reached across the table and took her hand. "I would never think less of you, Natashenka. You have a good soul."

She looked down at their joined hands. He couldn't tell what she was thinking. "My mother calls me that when she's upset, or when I'm upset. It's strange hearing it when I'm not upset."

"You're not?"

"No. Not at all. I don't understand what you told me, but there are strange things in this world I will never understand. I really loved dancing with you."

The non sequitur surprised him a bit. He gave her hand a gentle squeeze. "I loved dancing with you too. I haven't had much cause to have celebrations in my life. I take the opportunities that I can. I'm very happy you are here with me tonight."

"I'm happy I'm with you too, Patrick. I don't know who you are, really, but I know I'm safe with you."

He pulled away then. "No. You're not. If you or your baby were hurt because of who I am, I wouldn't be able to forgive myself. I told you that being pregnant wouldn't change your fellowship, but I don't think—" His words caught in his throat. She looked at him, her face a mask of confusion. "I'm afraid for you. I could have the city coroner take over your fellowship, I mean."

"No!" She jumped to her feet. She came around the table and threw her arms around his neck. "No, please don't."

He was surprised at her embrace, but he wrapped his arms around her waist. "It's dangerous to know me, the real me, Nataliya."

"I don't care," she said into his neck. Her breath was warm against his skin. "I don't care. I don't want to leave you. You look at me in a way that Alex never did. You are happy with a silly bag of presents. I want to show you what Christmas is all about. Please let me stay."

She pulled away enough to look at his eyes. She was straddling him, and she seemed to realize the odd position they were in. Her face flushed a bright red and she quickly moved off his lap. "I'm sorry. That was very forward of me. I'm sorry."

"I'm not," Patrick said. He already felt the loss of her warmth. He'd stiffened when she touched him, but he tensed more now that she was gone. He looked up at her. "It's your choice. To continue the fellowship with me. And to stay here and show me the Christmas movies I never got to see growing up."

She smiled at him. "What streaming services do you have?"

He let out an amused sigh. How quickly she moved from her fear of leaving him to showing him a Christmas movie. She was clearly nervous to ask more about his heritage, and he couldn't blame her. He stood up and led her into his living room. He had a large TV, a cozy couch, and a soft, fluffy blanket.

"Sit down," he said. "Do you want something else to drink?"

"Water for now," she said.

Patrick handed her the remote to the TV. "Find a movie, and I'll be right back."

He went into his kitchen and collapsed on the floor. He covered his face with his hands and took in several shuddering breaths. He'd never, ever revealed himself to anyone before. Even growing up, he didn't reveal his true nature to people. Everyone else thought he was a normal man, or discovered his identity on their own. Besides her initial reluctance to believe him, she didn't pry. Why wasn't she curious? Perhaps she was only humoring him. He looked up at the ceiling, feeling as if he were committing some sort of sin by keeping her in his house.

Patrick was tired of being alone. He was tired of walking through life with simple friendships and a handful of acquaintances he never spoke to. Nataliya had come into his life, her bright red hair like a beacon. He'd been drawn to her energy and her intelligent mind and her unbreakable spirit. He'd confessed to her, and she didn't seem to care. Perhaps the enormity of his identity was lost on her. Or she thought he was completely bonkers and she was just being kind.

He didn't know. He just didn't know. But she was still here, in his house, talking to him as if he were nothing more than a man. She'd jumped into his arms willingly, hugged him, danced with him, and he couldn't help but wonder about her own feelings. She was pregnant by another man, one that she didn't seem keen on being with. And she was in Patrick's home, wanting to be with him when she didn't have to be.

Patrick picked himself off the floor, got her a glass of water, and went into the living room to see White Christmas pulled up on the TV. Nataliya looked at him, a grin on her face. She'd pulled the soft blanket up on her lap.

"Come on, sit down! First *White Christmas*, then *Charlie Brown*, and maybe *Die Hard* if you're still awake," she said.

If she came to believe that he was who he said he was and she still wanted to watch Christmas movies, then she was a rare creature indeed.

Nataliya woke up sometime in the wee hours of the morning. The sound of a heartbeat let her know she was pressed against Patrick's chest. They'd both fallen asleep wrapped in blankets on the couch after their second movie. Patrick was warm, his breathing even and strong. He was alive. She kept her eyes closed, just listening to his heart. He was a living man. Was his father really Death? She couldn't explain anything, but she knew Patrick wasn't delusional. At least she didn't think he was.

She could so easily fall in love with Patrick. She wondered if it was fair of her to sleep in his arms, to give him gifts, to give him what she could have given Alex if he'd been half as attentive as Patrick. Was it even ethical? He was her mentor. But they were both adults, and they'd been through a harrowing experience together. She couldn't argue that they had an attraction for each other.

Nataliya wanted to fall in love with Patrick Morana. And Beck had implied that Patrick was most of the way there. Stranger things happened. It wasn't as if he were her instructor. They both knew it wasn't anything nefarious or coercive. It could certainly look as if he used his position over her, but that's the last thing he'd done. They hadn't even kissed, anyway.

She opened her eyes and saw the moonlight shining through the window, bathing the room in a beautiful glow. She gently extricated herself from Patrick's arms and got up to use the bathroom. She looked into the room she'd found him in when she first entered the house. The lights were on, so she went in. She sat down where he'd been and looked at the book that was left open.

Potion of Healing

A handwritten note rested on top of the page. The writing was in a language she couldn't understand. The symbols were strange, but they seemed to have a clear pattern. She flipped a few pages of the book. She found more potions, and only a few had similar handwritten notes. She went back to the potion of healing and saw a list of ingredients. Each corresponded with a jar on the table. The instructions said to grind them to a paste and spread liberally on the wound. The paste would dissolve into the wound and disappear, beginning a quick healing process.

She lifted the note from the page and tried to see if she could decipher anything. It was unlike any other language she'd seen. Besides Russian and English, she also knew French. She'd been interested in languages from a young age, being bilingual her entire life and trilingual by the time she graduated from high school. Latin had also been one of her interests, due to her medical education. She was fascinated by the ways languages had developed in different parts of the world. The symbols on these notes weren't like Nordic runes, or the pictographic characters of Chinese and Japanese. It wasn't Arabic, or Greek, or anything else she could think of. She would have looked it up on her phone, but she'd left it in the kitchen. She was about to pull out the photograph used as a bookmark when she heard a voice.

"It's called the Dead Tongue."

Nataliya looked up at Patrick. He stood in the doorway of the room, his hair a bit tousled from the pillow.

"The Dead Tongue?" she repeated.

"It's the same language that the rabisu screamed at me. It called me Son of Death. I'm curious, how were you able to see it? No one can see a rabisu latched onto the shoulders of a man."

"What do you mean? It just appeared from the dark, flying towards you," she answered. She remembered he'd said they could latch on to people, but she didn't make the connection between the rabisu and the rapist.

"Then it must have shed the Mantle of Darkness," he said, more to himself than to her. "It lost its power when I broke the man's arm and severed the connection." Most of what he'd said was lost on her. "Not many can speak or read the Dead Tongue. It's not often found in the land of the living." He took the book from her hands and closed it. He tucked the photograph further between the pages so no edges were visible, then set the book on an empty space on the bookshelf. "Russian is your first language, right?"

"Essentially. My parents spoke to me mostly in Russian, and I learned English through the neighborhood kids and school and day care. They learned English in ESL classes in Minneapolis. I was bilingual before my second birthday."

"The Dead Tongue was my first language," he said. "I didn't learn English until I was five." He spoke a few words that she didn't understand. A palpable energy made the air crackle. She jumped. "It's not for speaking lightly. Kind of like the Black Speech in *The Lord of the Rings*. Except it's not evil by nature. It's just the language of Death." He turned to face her, and something in the way he looked at her made her heart beat a bit faster.

"I don't know what's real anymore, Patrick," she said.

He shrugged. "Get used to it. I didn't think rabisu were real anymore. Though I suppose that's not what you meant. I'm sorry that you had to find all this out. In some ways it's safer that you don't know. Curiosity killed the cat, and though satisfaction brought it back, most of this isn't satisfying."

She didn't know how to reply to that. She wasn't sure whether she even wanted to know any of this, but it wasn't as if he'd told her unprovoked. "Beck told me not to ask about your family," she said finally.

"He doesn't know anything about it. But he's right. I don't like being asked about it. I never had a family in the sentimental sense of the word. Those Christmases you had? I didn't even really understand what those traditions were until I was practically a teenager." He shook his head.

"What about your mother?" she asked.

He started then, looking almost surprised that she would ask. She didn't care about Beck's advice, she wanted to know.

"I don't know her.

"Oh. I'm sorry. I suppose it's hard when they don't raise you." She only guessed, considering what he'd said.

"No, I mean I don't know who she is. No one ever told me. I don't think anyone besides my father knows." He shrugged.

"Who raised you then?"

Patrick left the room in silence. She was afraid she'd offended him, so she hurried to follow and apologize. He stood in the living room, turning off the TV and putting the cushions back on the couch. "It's late, Nataliya. You can sleep in my room and I'll sleep on the couch. I can call Beck to help me get my car from St. Charles tomorrow, if you have to leave. He'll take any excuse to get away from his family while his divorce is being finalized."

She knew the conversation was over at that moment. She wanted to know more, but Nataliya didn't dare ask. She also didn't try to apologize. It would be more awkward to bring it up. "Thank you for letting me stay here, Patrick."

"Thank you for thinking of me." He came around the couch and pulled her into his arms. "We haven't known each other very long, but I feel like I can trust you. I'd like to get to know you better, even though I try to keep to myself most of the time." He pulled away enough to look down into her eyes. It was dark, with only the moonlight streaming in. "I feel like you came here for a reason."

"Do you believe in fate, then?" she asked.

"I don't know, maybe. All I really understand is death. I don't understand families, or much about friendships. I've never been in love."

Nataliya tightened her arms around him. He had to be so lonely. "You're more than a boss to me, Patrick. I've only worked with you since October, but you're a good man. You're more than a friend. I don't really believe in fate. If it is real, then I'm glad it led me to you."

He squeezed her a bit, then let go. He led her to the bedroom, and before she realized it, he'd left her alone with a brush of his fingers through the ends of her hair like a kiss.

CHAPTER THIRTEEN

Christmas could go rot. He hated every aspect of the cheery light displays, the disgustingly fat Santas everywhere, and the excessive commercialization of every facet of life. Brian Peralta was a simple man, with simple pleasures, and pretending to tolerate his wife's utter devotion to the holiday was nigh on torture. If he had known the woman was a nut for stupid holidays, he would have never married her. She wasn't even religious. She just decorated the house and made shitty eggnog and dressed up their kids and their dog in garish red and green outfits. He drew the line at wearing a matching shirt in the family photos. A nice white button-down was the line.

This Christmas morning was by far the worst. He thought he'd escaped most of the kitsch when their youngest finally turned double digits, but then she'd gone and adopted another dog and devoted all her energy to matching up the dumb animals in costumes that cost more than he spent on fishing gear.

This year he was so fed up with the crappy cold weather and his wife's endless cheer that he didn't bother to feign appreciation for the gifts his three children gave him. His oldest son, who had come home from college, had given him nothing more than a gift subscription to a fishing magazine. One he already received. In spite of his hatred for the holiday, Brian felt very irritated at the thoughtless gift. While his wife finished cooking their big breakfast, Brian had left the house to walk the dogs, feeling more and more like slinking into his car on the pretense of driving to the lake and never coming back. Their neighborhood in South County was very well done up for the Christmas season, and he wanted to kick down every blow-up snowman he saw.

When he came back around the block, he thought he saw something moving in the shadow of the eaves above the front door. He blinked and rubbed at his eyes with one hand. Neither dog seemed to notice anything amiss. He climbed the stairs and grabbed the handle of the door. Before he turned it, something landed on his shoulders. He had a split second of sharp, intense, excruciating pain.

Then, it was gone. Brian grinned and went inside.

That evening, his in-laws found the bodies of his wife and three children and both of the dogs. There were no physical marks on any of the bodies.

Brian was nowhere to be found.

When the phone rang, Beck leaped out of his seat at the dinner table to answer it. His family all gave him long-suffering glances as he ran out of the room to talk in private.

"Detective Beck," he said, moving further into his mother's living room so no one could eavesdrop at the door.

"Hey Beck," said Elly, the dispatcher. "How's the fam?"

"Please, don't waste my time," Beck said with a bit of a bite in his voice. Elly liked teasing him, ever since they'd slept together soon after he kicked out his wife and he'd ended up crying the next morning. He couldn't look her in the eye since. "You're calling from the station. What's up?"

"You wanted me to keep you up to date on anything weird that might have happened."

"Yes? And? Spit it out, El."

"I'm getting to it. Is it that bad with your family?"

"My grandmother is ninety-seven and she keeps asking where Elise is. My brothers think it's funny, my sister keeps telling me how immoral divorce is, conveniently forgetting that the bitch cheated on me, and my mom keeps giving me these looks that say she's disappointed I haven't given her grandchildren yet, in spite of the fact that she has seven of them. Now, do you have something that can get me out of this rural hellhole or not?"

Elly laughed, but didn't stall any longer. "Four dead bodies were found in South County, along with two dead dogs. A mother and three children. They were found by the mother's parents. The husband is missing. His car is gone."

"Ooo, a family annihilator?" he asked.

"We don't know. There are no visible marks on the body, the bodies show signs of a struggle, but we don't know the causes of death yet. Dr. Morana is at the crime scene right now. I'll text you the address."

"God, it's going to take me at least an hour to get across the river," Beck said as he paced the living room.

"Do you want to hold off until later?"

"No! No. I'll get there as soon as I can. I want to talk to the forensics team as well. Thanks for the heads up, El."

"Sure, sure. Merry Christmas, asshole." She hung up on him. She was still a bit bitter that he never called her after they hooked up. And considering that they worked together, it made it worse.

He sighed and put his phone in his pocket. He dashed into his old bedroom and shoved his dirty clothes into his duffel. He was thankful he hadn't packed much.

"Jason! Jason, what's going on?"

His mother stood in the doorway, still wearing her Christmas apron.

"Work," he said, hauling the duffel bag on one shoulder. He went to grab his laptop bag.

"But you didn't finish dinner. And I made pecan pie especially for you."

"Mom, Elise was the one who liked pecan pie. I only tolerated it." He unplugged his phone charger. "I'm sorry I can't stay for eggnog, but I really have to go. Possible quadruple homicide."

His words didn't seem to affect his mother. She had her arms folded over her chest and a glare firmly in place.

"I specifically asked for you to spend the holidays here. You're always working. I'm afraid—"

"Mom! People are dead!" He was in no mood to be lectured by his mother. He would always be the disappointment of the family, and frankly, he didn't care. His brothers and sister all had kids. Even though he had a good and admirable job, the fact that Beck's marriage crumbled and he wasn't good enough to keep a woman from cheating apparently inflated his family's already negative view of him.

His mother scowled and crossed her arms. "That's no way to speak to me."

"Are you serious right now? I spent two days listening to everyone talk about how much they miss Elise. The woman cheated on me with her boss and then cheated on me again with a different guy when I took her back. That's not my fault, no matter what you think," Beck said, knowing his mother wouldn't understand at all. His parents had never had any of these problems, and when his father died, his mother had never even so much as thought about remarrying.

She unfolded her arms and gestured toward him. "It's because you run off at the first phone ring. That's why she stepped out. If you had just—"

"I don't give a shit," Beck interrupted. His desire to yell out his frustration had withered to a deadly calm. "I'm a failure. Yes, whatever, but I have a job to do. You don't care when Greg runs off when he has to respond to an emergency."

"He's a paramedic. Speed is important for that."

"And so is getting to a crime scene. The longer it takes to find a murderer, the less likely it is that we ever will. I can't spend time arguing with you. I have to go."

"Fine. Fine! Ruin Christmas!" She threw her hands up in the air.

Beck rolled his eyes and stepped past her. "Is it really ruining it when none of you even care about me? I'm thirty-four years old, and you still treat me like I'm twelve. Have a good night. Merry Christmas. Tell Grandma that Elise cheated on me, for the love of God."

Beck left the house, his heart beating fast. He did not expect to get into a fight with his mother this Christmas. He had been content to spike whatever hot drink was given to him and spend the week eating and hiking around the tree farm. But the emotions simmering under the surface had exploded, and his family's preference for his ex-wife was made clear. Though his words to his mother were true, he also felt glad to investigate a crime scene even though he wasn't on duty. Because if he had to deal with five more days of that, he was going to drink his brother Greg's entire liquor cabinet.

Driving back to Missouri at a perfectly legal speed, he got there later than he'd told Elly, but the scene still crawled with cops and the CSU. To his surprise, Patrick was still there, standing with Nataliya on the sidewalk in front of the house.

"You made it," Patrick said.

"I thought you'd be here and gone by now," Beck said.

"It took us a while to get here," Patrick said with a shrug. Beck glanced from him to Nataliya. She wore a sheepskin coat and her hair was tied back. She looked pale, but it was dark and she was a redhead. "And then we decided to wait till you got here."

Beck nodded and walked up the path to the front door. "Did you determine COD?" he asked.

Both examiners followed him, and Patrick answered, "No, but we're hoping to do the autopsies over the next couple of days. A vet is going to necropsy the dogs as well. Could be poison."

"Wouldn't be the first time a family annihilator went nuts on a holiday. Poison is an unusual choice for a man, though," Beck said. He nodded at one of his officers standing at the door and walked in. "Agent Lyons would probably know more."

"When is she coming back?" Nataliya asked.

"Tomorrow, I think," he said. "She was going to stay through New Year's Eve, but apparently her family isn't any better than mine." They had that in common. They'd exchanged a few terse texts, and he'd sent her a message before he'd left the farm. She, like him, had wanted any excuse to get out of her family's clutches. Murder was always good for that, whether committing it or investigating it.

The house was dark. The three bodies lay right there in the front room, with the Christmas tree lights illuminating them. The mother was the closest, with her whole body twisted up on the ground. Nothing looked broken, but the angle wasn't natural. It was as if she'd been struggling and died suddenly in the middle of it. Whatever she'd been struggling with had gotten up and left her there. The three kids were at various points of the room. The youngest, a boy probably about ten or eleven, held one of the dogs in his arms next to the tree. His eyes were open and glassy. The next oldest was a girl of about thirteen, and she too held one of the dogs. She lay at the foot of the couch, as if hiding behind it from the front door. The third was the eldest son, late teens. He lay in the middle of the floor, like he was posed, with his hands crossed on his midsection. His hair was a mess, though, and his expression was not one of peace. It was slack.

Other than the bodies, nothing seemed out of place. Toys and other gifts were strewn about the room, with pieces of wrapping paper and ribbon forgotten in the cleanup. Beck wandered throughout the house. Breakfast, uneaten, sat on the table. One of the CSU was taking photos.

"The oven was still on," she said when she noticed him. "Looks like she just took the breakfast casserole out of the oven and didn't have a chance to turn it off before everything happened."

"If they didn't eat breakfast, then I wonder if it was poison," Beck said.

"Could be, if they had anything to drink when they opened presents. We're checking the dishwasher for dishes once we get photos here." The woman nodded at him and continued taking photos. He returned to the front room, where Patrick and Nataliya investigated the bodies.

"It's hard to tell," Nataliya said. She was crouched beside a body, her arm in front of her nose as if she smelled something. The bodies hadn't begun to rot yet, though. "But do you think. . ." She trailed off when she saw Beck.

"I don't know. We'll have to open them up." Patrick stood up and went around the mother to help Nataliya to her feet. Beck watched it all with interest. Had they hooked up? They certainly looked more familiar with each other than before. He had wondered how long it would be before they got to it. He smiled. Oh, Julie was definitely going to be paying up.

"CSU still needs to do more work here," Beck said, noting that they hadn't finished combing through the room. "So you two can go on back to doing whatever it was you were doing before you got called here."

"What do you mean by that?" Nataliya asked, her face flushed. Beck nearly chuckled.

"Get your mind out of the gutter, Beck," Patrick muttered. "Last night we caught the rapist."

"What?!" Beck exclaimed. "Why didn't anyone tell me?"

"We were busy giving our statements, I guess, and then we forgot," Patrick replied. "I don't know why your chief didn't tell you."

"I would have come back as soon as I heard that! And then I wouldn't have had to listen to sermon after sermon about how I'm going to hell because I'm getting a divorce!" Beck wanted to shout in frustration, but throwing a tantrum in front of four dead bodies seemed kind of tacky.

Though insinuating that the coroner and his fellow were doing it was probably even tackier.

"Sorry," Patrick said nonchalantly. "I can tell you more when you're done here."

"Yeah. I gotta interview the neighbors. They're starting to gather." He looked out the window to see people on the street pressing against the crime scene tape around the lawn.

"We'll leave you to it," Patrick said. "We'll probably be at the morgue by the time you're done."

"I'll drop in when I can." Beck nodded at Nataliya. "Sorry for being a jackass. Again."

Nataliya smirked. "Ah, but you can't help it." He knew he was not forgiven. He shook his head. Not that he cared. He didn't want to be mean to her, but he was too used to speaking his mind since his personal life imploded.

Probably not the best way to go about investigating homicides.

CHAPTER FOURTEEN

"Brian has always been polite, but distant."

Beck glanced over his notebook at the old woman. Jennifer Randolph, mother of the dead woman, grandmother to the dead kids. "Distant?" he asked.

"I guess I never understood what Sarah saw in him. I don't think he really loved her. He has a good job, provided a good house, and took them on wonderful vacations." The woman dabbed at her eyes with a handkerchief. "But he never showed any warmth to her or the children. He acted like it was a chore to pay attention to any of them. Still, he was never violent, he never yelled or hit them. He even treated the dogs well. I can't believe he could have done this, Detective."

Beck licked his lips. The other officers were interviewing the neighbors. He looked at Mr. Randolph, who paced back and forth with his hands in his white hair. Mr. Randolph hadn't been able to calm down enough to speak to anyone, not even his wife. Beck couldn't really blame the man. They'd just discovered their only daughter and their three grandchildren were dead. With Brian missing, it looked very suspicious.

"We're still trying to determine the cause of death," Beck said. Though he was pretty sure it wasn't some random carbon monoxide leak. The house had already been checked for it anyway. "Did you know of any other problems in the family?"

Mrs. Randolph let out a shuddering sigh. "I know that Brian was having a hard time with Joey. The oldest. Joey never really got along with Brian, I suppose," she said. She twisted the handkerchief between her hands. "But Joey's a teenager. I mean, was a teenager." She sniffed. "Teenagers are supposed to give their parents a hard time, right?"

Beck didn't know if he was supposed to answer that.

"Christmas isn't Brian's favorite holiday, but I didn't think he hated it," she continued. "I wouldn't put it past him to drive off for a few days to get away from it all. But not today. Not on Christmas Day."

"Do you know if Brian was having any difficulties at work? Or with his friends? Could he be seeing another woman?"

Mrs. Randolph untwisted her handkerchief. "I don't know, Detective. Brian and I were never close. He spoke to me only when he had to. He talked even less to my husband. Sarah never said anything either. As far as I know, everything was normal. Oh, Detective," she cried out. "My poor baby girl!" She buried her face into her damp handkerchief and began sobbing. Mr. Randolph hurried over and pulled his wife into his embrace.

"I'll leave you alone now," Beck said. He held out his business card. "If you can think of anything, anything at all, please give me a call. We'll be searching the whole house for any possible clue as to what's going on, and we put an APB out on his truck. We'll find him."

"Thank you, Detective Beck," Mr. Randolph said. Beck nodded and headed off to meet one of the other detectives standing by a squad car.

"None of the neighbors know anything," Harper said. She looked tired, and her blonde hair was slipping out of her ponytail. She was newer on the force, and not long out of college. Beck didn't work with her much, as he spent most of his time working with Julie on the rape cases. "They all said he's a private guy. Doesn't really talk to anyone, doesn't join in neighborhood barbecues. Doesn't play outside with his kids, his wife mows the lawn. This guy is closed off."

"The in-laws said the same thing. He's cold, reserved, and by the sound of it, the lamest douche in the universe." Beck closed his notepad and put it in his pocket. The night had grown bitterly cold, and he wanted to get back to the station and warm up. The transporters were in the process of bagging the bodies in the house, and the Randolphs watched. He wasn't going to judge, at least he shouldn't. He had no idea how he'd react in their place. "Hopefully Morana can figure out how they died."

"Talk about a kick in the teeth. Merry Christmas, four people are mysteriously dead, along with their two dogs." Harper shook her head. "Really makes you grateful for what you do have."

"I suppose." Beck didn't hate his family. He kind of wished he did. It would make it easier. But he always felt like he had to make his mom proud of him. It was Christmases like this one that he desperately missed his dad. "Bad luck getting called up on Christmas, eh?"

Harper shrugged. "I guess I'd rather it be me than one of the officers who has a spouse and kids. I thought you were in Illinois until New Year's."

"Yes, well, duty calls." Beck stamped his feet. "I'm freezing my ass off. I'm gonna head back to the station. I'll see you there."

Harper nodded. "I'll make sure we get the rest of the statements or arrange to get them tomorrow morning."

"Thanks. Good work." Beck left her to finish up at the crime scene and went to his car. He sat for a moment as the car warmed up. He pulled out his cell phone and texted Julie.

There's something very weird about this new case. Not conclusively homicide, shares many traits with family annihilators. Husband seems to be an emotionally repressed asshole. And not in a me way, in a will-totally-snap-and-kill-his-entire-family way. No one seemed to have seen it coming, if it was a homicide. Patrick and Talya seemed kind of . . . intimate when I saw them. So who knows with them. But he couldn't say anything about COD just looking at them.

Something wasn't adding up and he couldn't completely connect the dots. He knew family annihilators often killed their entire family including pets, often on significant holidays. Julie must have been awake still, as she texted him back fairly quickly.

Family annihilators usually kill for three reasons. 1. Paranoia, as in trying to kill the family to keep them safe. 2. If the economic status suddenly changes, such as if he loses a job or loses everything gambling. Or 3. If he finds himself disappointed with some aspect of family life such as a cheating spouse, or if he was cheating and wanted a different family life. I'll be back in St. Louis late tomorrow, as I couldn't get an earlier flight. But check the missing husband for those three motives if it does turn out to be a homicide. Hopefully when Patrick can determine COD, we'll have more answers. And how intimate were they? Like just had Holly Jolly Christmas Sex or was it awkward twelve-year-old puppy-love intimacy? Because we all know from your experience that a 'hit it and quit it' results in everyone pretty much hating you and not wanting to be anywhere near you.

Beck harrumphed to himself when he read the last bit of the text. "Ha ha," he said to the steering wheel. "Very funny." He composed a quick text before finally heading to the station.

All three are possible until we get digging into their finances and personal lives. And Intimate as in I thought they might have banged but they probably just cuddled while watching White Christmas. See you tomorrow.

Patrick sat on the stool next to the autopsy table. The youngest child was in place, the block under his shoulders and his chest cavity opened. Patrick removed his gloves and stared at the body. The fourth autopsy. The fourth crushed heart.

He and Nataliya had performed autopsies on the mother and oldest son as soon as they arrived at the morgue. Utterly exhausted, the two went their separate ways to get some good sleep. No matter what Beck had thought, they hadn't arrived at the crime scene together. After Nataliya woke up on Christmas morning, they ate a simple breakfast, which was only a fraction more awkward than he'd expected, and then Nataliya went home to prepare herself to speak to Alex's parents and her own. As far as Patrick knew, the crime scene call happened after she told them she was pregnant. But she didn't say one way or the other.

They both arrived at the morgue at noon the day after Christmas, having gotten a few scant hours of sleep after spending so much time doing the autopsies. Nataliya had taken a break after the first autopsy of the day, and he couldn't blame her. He tried to get her to go home to sleep, but instead she stayed at the morgue to sleep on the couch in the break room. He'd done the youngest child's autopsy on his own. He knew by then what to expect.

With the except of sexual assault, all four members of the Peralta family had the exact same findings as the four rape victims. The ones who'd been murdered by the rabisu.

Patrick stared at the body of the young boy. He wondered if he could have done more to stop the rabisu. He didn't know how to kill one. He had no idea it had even been there when he attacked the rapist. He needed to talk to Beck, to see what he could find on the rapist, and if he had even intended on killing the young women. Patrick had no idea what a rabisu could do, but it was definitely possible that it had enough sway over the rapist's mind to put into action something he might not have had the stomach to do before. Murder was never done unless the murderer wanted it to happen. Whether or not the murderer was capable of crushing hearts was another story. He knew enough about death to understand that people died in a lot of ways, intentional or not, and no one's mind could be possessed enough to kill another human being if they had never had such inclinations. A demon wouldn't possess a moral person and cause him to commit ghastly murders.

Patrick looked up at the storage refrigerator. The soul of the eldest son stood in front of where his body was held. This was the second time the soul of the rabisu's victim lingered. It was unnerving. The young man had been handsome in life, and in death he looked angry. His eyes were dark, and he glared at Patrick. He didn't try to speak, not like the

Jane Doe. Souls almost always knew they were dead, from what Patrick had seen over the years, and this boy knew he was dead. The soul was more animated than he was used to, as well. It looked at the young boy, and his anger turned to one of anguish. The soul moved its arm.

Patrick nearly fell out of his chair in shock. Souls never moved. They just stood, looking at him. To move its arm like that?

"Who are you?" Patrick asked, his voice a breath below a whisper.

The soul kept his hand out toward his brother. It folded its fingers in until it pointed straight at the boy.

Patrick turned back to the child in front of him. He'd never had a soul communicate so much with him. A mere pointing of a finger, but that was more than any had ever done before. The child's heart had collapsed, only it seemed much more mangled, if such a thing were possible. It held no shape, and the only reason Patrick knew it was the heart was because of the location in the body.

Conversely, the oldest brother's heart had been less mangled. From what Patrick could tell, the boy had been an athlete. His heart had been strong, much stronger than his younger brother's.

Patrick looked at the young boy's heart again. Something was different. Not that it was more mangled. He put on a new pair of gloves and started to dissect it. He pieced it back to rights, and as he did so, he noticed that there was something wrong with the boy's heart. Something that had nothing to do with it being crushed.

Nataliya came into the room as he was finishing up. "What did you find?" she asked.

"Tricuspid atresia," Patrick said. "It was a devil to figure it out. This boy died before his heart was crushed. I bet if we checked the tissues more carefully, we'll see he died of lack of oxygen. Once I saw the heart, I stopped looking for anything else abnormal." Patrick motioned for Nataliya to turn off the video camera, which she did immediately. He looked over at the soul, who had dropped his hand. He didn't look angry anymore. But he was still there, watching.

"What's going on, Patrick? Something else you don't want on the record?"

"It's the rabisu. I can't figure out how it's killing without leaving a mark. This boy's defect must have caused cardiac arrest. Maybe he was scared, I don't know. But it caused him to die. His heart was crushed just like the others. Regardless, I'm certain the rabisu attached itself to the father." Patrick let out a heavy breath.

Nataliya looked at the heart. He still couldn't tell if she believed him or not, but she seemed more inclined to listen to what he was saying. "Are you saying this kid probably saw his family killed?" she asked.

Patrick nodded. "I know so. The first one killed was the oldest son."

"How do you know?"

"I know, Nataliya. It's one of those things that I just know. I can feel it. I am born of death. I know it as intimately as a friend. The death order is the oldest son, the mother, the daughter, and the youngest son. Then the dog the little boy was holding, then the other dog. I bet anything that when the vet gets back to us their hearts will be crushed too."

Nataliya looked up at him. "Okay," she said. "So what can we do about it? We can't just tell Julie and Beck that an ancient Mesopotamian demon is possessing people and using their bodies to kill."

Patrick looked at the soul again. The boy looked at him, his eyes sad this time. "Julie knows things. I don't know about Beck, but we can trust Julie."

"She knows?"

"Some things. She doesn't know who I really am. I didn't think to tell you. It's been a very strange couple of days. Nataliya, can you please go to the office and get some more paper?"

Nataliya gave him a strange look but did as he asked. He turned back to the soul.

"My father is coming for you," Patrick said. "Please, go with him. Pay the Ferryman. You'll find the coins in your hand."

The soul didn't move, but it was clear he heard Patrick.

"I will do everything I can to find your father and stop him."

The boy opened his mouth, but no sound came.

"When you see the girls, tell them I'm sorry. You'll know who I'm talking about. The other victims of the rabisu will find you, I promise. Tell them," his voice caught in his throat before he could continue, "Tell them I'm sorry that I couldn't save them. I didn't know what this evil thing was. And I'm going to stop it now. Please let them know that."

The soul disappeared. Patrick fought the urge to cry. He spoke for the dead, but he couldn't save them.

CHAPTER FIFTEEN

Beck nursed his cup of coffee as he peered over at Patrick. "I finally got the video of his interrogation," he said.

Patrick, who sat on the opposite side of Beck's desk, sighed in relief. "Good. Is it all right if I watch it?"

Beck nodded. He opened his laptop. "Yeah. I was going to show Julie but she isn't getting back into town until after ten tonight." After a few moments of clicking through his email, he pulled up the video. "I wish they'd let me do the interview, but I was technically on vacation when they apprehended him. The police in St. Charles handled the original arrest and questioning, but he's going to be charged for the rapes and murders."

He turned the laptop around and pulled his chair out to sit next to Patrick so he could watch it as well. "I haven't seen it yet," he added. "I called you as soon as it came into my email."

Patrick didn't say anything, so Beck hit play.

On the video, a man about thirty years old sat in an interview room. He was dark-haired, with dark eyes. The video quality was terrible, but the man looked tired. A male detective sat across from him, along with another police officer. After some of the preliminary talk about rights and asking if the man wanted a lawyer and understood the charges against him, they started in on the questioning. Interviews weren't usually very dramatic, but this one was shorter than Beck had expected, considering the man never asked for a lawyer.

"Can you tell me what happened earlier tonight?" the detective asked.

The man kept his face down, staring at the table. He licked his lips and shrugged one shoulder. His other shoulder was inhibited by a sling, courtesy of Patrick breaking his arm.

"You were found attacking Ms. Gordon in the alley. Can you explain what you were doing?"

"What do you think I was doing?" the suspect asked, still not looking up.

"You were attempting to sexually assault a young woman."

"I wasn't trying to hurt her," he said, his voice almost too quiet. "It wasn't supposed to be like that. None of them were supposed to be like that."

"What do you mean it wasn't supposed to be like that?" the detective asked.

"She wasn't supposed to fight. She was supposed to want it." He repeated both sentences again. "She was supposed to like it."

The detective tapped his pen on his notepad. "Why did you continue if she was supposed to like it? She clearly didn't."

The man looked up at him for the first time. His face was ghoulishly pale in the poor video quality. "I thought it would work. I knew it would work eventually. That's what's supposed to happen. Every time, it was supposed to work. I gave them the drink, but they spit it out, so I forced it down."

If the detective was as confused as Beck, he didn't make that obvious to the suspect. "What drink did you give them?"

The man put his head down on the table, his hands gripping his hair. "I thought it would make them love me. It lied to me. I thought I could get them to love me. None of them loved me." His voice rambled on quietly, too quiet to hear on the video. Then he started sobbing, his words even more incoherent.

"What is he saying?" Patrick asked, leaning forward.

Beck was just as mystified. "Did he try to drug them?" he asked.

"What was in the drink?" the detective asked. "Please, calm down. We need to know what was in the drink."

"Water," the man said, lifting his head slightly. He let out a wet cough. "Ragweed." He coughed again and wiped at his eyes. "Cloves. Dill. Tulips and jasmine."

"Ragweed? What the hell?" Beck leaned in as well.

"Witch hazel," Patrick murmured at the same time as the suspect.

Beck's attention was torn away from the interrogation. He stared at Patrick, a sense of unease creeping over him as he looked at his friend. Patrick still leaned forward, peering in concentration at the video.

"They were supposed to love me," the man said again, his voice wobbly. "But none of them did. They all fought back. It told me, in my head, that they'd love me. And when they fought back, it told me that they were all wrong. They deserved to die. So it killed them. I wanted them to die because none of them would have ever bothered to look at me twice. They tried to kill me first, so I killed them instead. None of this worked like it was supposed to. I just wanted to have someone love me but they all hated me so I had to kill him." He shoved his fists against his closed eyes and said, "It sank into my heart. When I saw her, it came from somewhere above me and clawed its way in. And I saw her, and gave her the drink I'd made. And she threw it back at me so I shoved it down her throat. It was nighttime in the Central West End. And she tried to kick and bite me. And it told me to kill her. I don't remember how I killed her."

"We need to get a psych eval," the police officer said, just loud enough for the camera to pick up the sound.

The detective nodded. "Yeah. He's rambling nonsense." The camera switched off.

Beck and Patrick sat in silence for a long moment. Then, Patrick stood up. "I have to go. Tell Julie to call me as soon as she gets in."

He left the station before Beck could say a word.

Julie looked from Patrick to the door. "Are you serious?" she asked. Patrick didn't bother to answer. He stepped in front of her and knocked on the door. Julie would have rolled her eyes if she hadn't been wearing sunglasses. She'd barely been in St. Louis eight hours and already she was back on the case of whatever was crushing people's hearts.

She'd been dead asleep when Patrick called her, informing her that he knew exactly what had been terrorizing girls. The developments in the case were startling, to say the least. Now she was wearing her work suit, pumped so full of coffee she'd probably vomit before the day was out, and wondering how the hell they were supposed to find information in the house before them.

It wasn't a house. It was a literal mansion. Julie had gone to some pretty interesting places since she'd become a federal agent. Mansions and expensive homes were normal in DC, and the bigger a space was in NYC, the more expensive. But she was used to spending the past few months in St. Louis, where the cost of living was remarkably low and people had surprisingly liberal sensibilities in some respects but still went fishing on the weekends to the Lake of the Ozarks. Of course St. Louis had wealthy neighborhoods, but this seemed excessive. The gate had been open, so Patrick had driven right up to the front door. The house was surrounded by trees, a veritable oasis in the middle of the city. However most of them had lost their leaves, so it looked rather creepy. A green Lamborghini was parked in the driveway in front of their car.

"Who the hell do you know that lives here?" Julie asked.

Again Patrick didn't answer. He knocked on the door a second time.

"They probably already know we're here," Julie said. "You can't tell me this place doesn't have security cameras."

"Of course they have them. And knocking is the polite thing to do." Patrick's smirk told her that he was enjoying this. It seemed a bit at odds with his usual personality. Maybe he was finally warming up to her.

Very soon, the door was opened by a short woman wearing holey jeans, fuzzy purple slippers, and a Cardinals T-shirt. "It's cold, get the hell inside." She took Patrick's arm and hauled him in. Julie was taken aback that a woman who probably weighed one hundred and ten pounds soaking wet managed to manhandle the six foot well-built man with ease. She followed the two inside, and the woman closed the door. Julie took off her sunglasses. Her attention was drawn to the small woman. She looked younger than Julie had expected, probably mid-twenties. Her hair was dyed purple and was tied up in a surprisingly neat bun. She didn't wear any jewelry except a wedding ring that had a blue stone.

"I haven't seen you in ages," the woman said to Patrick, slugging him on the arm. "What's with the fed?"

"Liv, this is Special Agent Julie Lyons. She's been working on the case. Julie, this is Olivia Masters."

Liv looked Julie up and down. "Huh. Didn't expect an actual Fox Mulder." She grinned. "Come on." She led the trio further into the house, and Julie couldn't help but be flabbergasted. She'd thought Dr. Paulson's wedding had been opulent. This house was absolutely insane. Marble floors, wooden staircases, huge, arching windows, and vaulted ceilings. Liv led them through a doorway that was closed with an actual wrought-iron gate. They took a couple of steps down into a library with wood floors, a fire blazing in the fireplace, and several windows showing the bleak outdoors. Dark wood beams crossed the ceiling, and a chandelier burned brightly. There were a couple of cozy reading chairs by the fire, along with a large mahogany table in the middle of the room. There was a silver tea set on it, along with several old books in a neat pile, a purple notebook, pens, and a large potted verbena plant. The tiny, delicate flowers were purple. Julie was noticing a theme.

"Please, sit," Liv said. She gestured at the table. "Would you like anything to drink?"

"Tea is fine," Patrick said. Julie shook her head. They all sat down at the table and Liv poured tea for herself and Patrick.

"So. These murders. You were very scant on details, Paddy." Liv smiled and took a sip of the steaming tea.

"Don't call me that," Patrick said. "And I couldn't tell you because the case is currently under investigation and many details have been intentionally withheld from the media."

"And you don't trust me?" Liv's blue eyes sparkled over the rim of her teacup.

"Not hardly," Patrick said with a half-smile. "But that's beside the point. I need your help."

"I've been waiting to hear you say that." Liv glanced at Julie. "So you brought her? Is she your girlfriend?"

"Not hardly," Julie said, echoing him. He glared at her. "His interests lie elsewhere."

"Oh?!" Liv leaned forward. "Do tell! Is it a redhead? I always figured a redhead would be the one to catch his eye."

"Why, yes, it—"

Patrick interrupted. "That is not the topic of discussion I came for!"

Both Julie and Liv turned to look at him. Liv put down her teacup and said, "You're seriously not going to let me find out more about this mysterious person? Is it a man or a woman? I thought maybe it would be a man, you know."

"I'm not gay," Patrick said in a flat voice. "For the last time."

"Why are you so offended?" Liv asked.

"You know I'm not offended and that I don't care what you think of me. If you're going to make predictions, at least get the details right." Patrick let out a heavy sigh. "I knew better than to come here."

Liv grinned. "And still you came. You just missed me so much."

"So, why did we come here, Patrick?" Julie asked finally.

"I told you, she can help us. If she shuts up about my love life." He glared at Liv, who just winked.

"Fine, fine. In the spirit of Christmas, I'll shut up," Liv conceded.

"Christmas was two days ago," Julie said.

"Au contraire, Agent Lyons." Liv turned her smile to Julie. "If you want to be technical, the month leading up to the twenty-fifth of December was Advent. The twenty-fifth is the first day of Christmas. Then you have the twelve days of Christmas, like in the song, up till January 6th. That is Epiphany, traditionally the celebration of when the Magi came to Jesus with gifts."

"In addition to being a religious historian," Patrick said, "She's also religious herself."

"You?" Julie looked at the young woman again. She already looked out of place in a house worth millions, but with her purple hair, multiple ear piercings, and her general attitude, Julie didn't see it.

"Appearances can be deceiving, am I right, Paddy?"

Paddy frowned. "Don't call me that. I'm almost certain of the creature that killed the women."

"Please, tell me. I've been waiting all morning." Liv took another sip of tea.

"Rabisu," Patrick said.

"Seriously? Akkadian mythology, that's something you don't hear every day." Liv put down her teacup and wandered to one of the walls of books and pulled one out. "*The Religion of Babylonia and Assyria* by Theophilus G. Pinches. Published"—she opened the book's cover—"1906. Let's see, rabisu." She flipped a few pages. "'The rabisu is regarded as a spirit which lay in wait to pounce upon his prey.' That's all? Hmm." She put the book back and pulled out another. She read a few pages, then put it back. "It's not as vampiric as you might think. It doesn't suck blood, or even really suck energy. It seems to be associated with nightmares." She picked a third book and brought it over to the table. It was much larger than the other two. "*Daemones*. Never formally published by any printing press. The first manuscript was written during the Siege of Antioch during the First Crusade. Decades later, it was copied by the monks in an abbey near that city.

This copy is a fair reproduction of those illuminated copies, produced only two hundred years ago."

"Do you really know where all your books come from?" Julie asked.

"More or less." Obviously Liv didn't think anything was all that strange about it. She opened the book, and Julie was amazed by the illumination on each page. In spite of the horrific displays of demons, the colors and script were beautiful. Liv flipped a few more pages. "I don't actually read Latin all that well, but that's what translator apps are for. Here we go, rabisu."

Before she could pull out her phone, Patrick took the book and seemed to be reading it.

"You read Latin?" Julie asked.

"Sort of," he said.

"Sort of?" Julie looked at Liv.

"Patrick is a man of many talents," the young woman replied.

After a few very long moments, Patrick spoke. His words came out slow, and it was clear he was translating as he read. "The rabisu lurks at the door. Those who cannot master their sinful urges will fall prey. Their acts are of their own intent, but might not have been taken had the rabisu not attached to his shoulders. Keep your head up, as God said to Cain, who murdered his brother. The demon of urges, the demon who squeezes the life muscle of man to destruction. A shadow figure, no, a shadowy figure, with eyes that glow without color, and the size of the bird of death—I think that's a vulture—and who can only be removed from this space—no, life—existence?—by the presence of Verum Mortem. Verum Mortem," he repeated.

"True Death," Liv said.

Patrick continued translating. "Once the presence is felt, the rabisu will flee, for it does not want to return to the Desert of Anguish. It enjoys sending souls to the Road of Bone, and the Ferryman knows these souls by their eyes." He stopped reading and looked up at Liv. "There is no Desert of Anguish."

"I know," Liv said. Her voice was soft.

Patrick rubbed his hands over his face and he read. "The rabisu craves to end the lives of the innocent. It will not stop until it is banished and the judgment of Letum—who is Letum—" He stopped short. "Liv."

"Letum is another term for Mors," Liv said.

"Mors?" Julie asked.

"I know that," Patrick snapped, and it was perhaps the rudest Julie had ever seen him. She stared at him in shock. "Thanatos, the Greek God of Death. Let me finish, I'm almost done. Once Verum Mortem has touched the rabisu, for it is not weak against this creature, the rabisu can be flung down past Cocytus so that its lamentations will be held forever more away from the Children of God." He put down the book. "Who wrote this book, Liv?"

"One of the warrior monks," she replied. "The Knights Templar wouldn't be formed for another twenty years, but he was one of the precursors. Eudes the Fair. His name is mostly lost to the greater history of the Crusades, but his work is well known in my circles."

"In religious history?" Julie asked.

"My other circles. Like Patrick here. Though he doesn't usually read old texts. He's too busy cracking open bodies."

Patrick didn't respond. He stared at the book in front of him, and Julie noticed that he looked deeply troubled by the pages.

"So this thing is causing the deaths through a human," Julie said. "How is it killing these people without making a mark?"

"A lot of dark creatures can kill without touching," Liv said. "Demons can't kill on their own. They need a host."

"A rabisu isn't a true demon," Patrick said. "I saw it. It's just a hideous monster."

"Yes, I know," Liv replied. "Not a fallen angel, but some other evil creature. Eudes the Fair called it a demon because he didn't realize there was a difference in what he discovered. Regardless, he wrote about it. He had to have seen it."

"The fact that a rabisu is real means this isn't a fanciful book of myths," Patrick said. He glanced at Julie. "But I've never encountered it before."

"I'm not surprised. I've never even heard of anyone else seeing one," Liv said. "They aren't fallen angels, but many creatures in many myths and religions have abilities to influence humans. That's why the rapist was urged on to make the supposed love potions. He might not have tried if the rabisu wasn't on his shoulders, pulling out his basest desires." Liv gestured toward the stack of books next to the tea set. "Everything from demonic possession to the obscure, dead society myths show that evil is a liar. What's curious is how it turned from rape to murder."

"The rapist said he wanted the girls dead when they wouldn't fall in love with him," Julie said. Beck had sent her a copy of the interrogation, and she'd watched it several times on the plane. "It told him to kill them, but he doesn't remember how he killed them."

"Intent," Liv said, shaking her head. "It's rare, but intent, combined with the influence of evil, can do a lot."

"Are you saying the sheer will of the rapist's desires crushed the girls' hearts?" Patrick said.

"Yes. But it has to be in certain conditions," Liv explained. "We all think rash thoughts. Someone cuts us off in traffic, we curse at them. We want to kill someone who cheated us. All those things." She held her hands up in a shrug. "But we don't really want someone cursed, or dead. In fact, most of us would be horrified if we expressed a wish for someone to die and then they actually did die. Even murderers often feel regret for their crimes of passion. But the ones who don't feel the regret? That's when the rabisu can work. The rapist, and Brian Peralta, truly wanted their victims dead. And in the heat of the moment, the rabisu used their intent. It's magic. It's evil. And it worked."

Patrick bit his lip. "Liv, I need to figure out how to find it."

"You?" Julie asked. "No, Patrick, it's too dangerous."

"Too dangerous? So I should just leave it up to you?" Patrick licked his lips, as if he were going to say something.

Julie interrupted him. "You have a safe job, Patrick. You're very good at what you do, as well. Leave this to people who signed up for the danger."

Patrick laughed, which was the exact opposite of what she was expecting. She looked at Liv, who stood up and sauntered over to one of the bookshelves. She didn't seem too interested in the conversation.

"What's so funny?" Julie asked.

"Just the idea that you think you can capture this thing and get rid of it."

Julie didn't like that Patrick was laughing at her. He always seemed so polite. And she knew a lot more than he'd given her credit for, even after she revealed her knowledge to him. "And how do you know I can't?" she asked.

"Because you're not Verum Mortem," Liv said. She picked up an ornate box carved from some type of black wood. She walked over to the table and opened it. "And only Verum Mortem can touch a rabisu and not fall under its power." She lifted up a necklace and held it out to Patrick. "This will hide your nature. I want it back. It costs more than your life."

"My life is worth a lot, Liv. You know that."

"Yes. And my point still stands." She handed the necklace over to Patrick. The thin leather cord had a strange glass bauble strung on it. Inside the glass was a dried yellow flower and a dark pink sparkling dust inside. He tilted it so the dust revealed a very tiny bone. "That's a coppery thorntail leg bone," Liv explained. "Very, very rare extinct hummingbird. It also has red beryl dust and a snapdragon blossom."

"How'd you get that?" Julie asked.

"I have ways. I'm lucky enough that I married a man who has contacts around the world. He comes from old money, but we have made quite a pretty penny trading in certain items." Liv took something else out of the box. "I think you'll find this useful as well." She handed Patrick a long, brown and white striped feather. Something small was tied to the shaft, but Julie couldn't tell what it was.

"Where did you find that?" Patrick asked, though his tone was more flabbergasted than Julie's had been.

"It took a lot, and I mean a *lot*, of searching," Liv replied. "The owl died naturally, which is the only way that the feathers can be used for that talisman."

"Can I ask what that is?" Julie felt a bit out of place. These two people seemed to be talking about something else now.

"That talisman calls Death," Liv said.

"Death? Like, to kill someone?"

"No. As in the personification." Liv closed the lid of the box. "Death doesn't always answer. But whoever holds that talisman has a greater chance of succeeding."

Julie glanced at Patrick. He held the feather in front of him. "I don't need this," he said, holding it back at Liv.

"You asked me about it last year. I thought you still wanted it."

"I'm sorry if you went to the effort on my behalf. I couldn't afford it anyway." Patrick pushed it further toward Liv. She took it and put it back in the box.

"Don't worry about the trouble, I can turn it around again very easily. I'm just surprised. You were very interested in finding it."

Patrick shrugged. "I don't need it right now. Thank you for the amulet." He slipped it on over his head. "Do you have anything that can help me find the rabisu to begin with? It was sheer luck that I even found it the first time."

"Was it?" Liv asked. "You told me the rapist wasn't from St. Charles, isn't that right?"

"Yeah, he was from the city," Julie replied for Patrick.

"The man was going north, then came back down, which speaks to some randomness. But the fact that you were the one who saw it in the alley in the middle of an attempted crime? There are no coincidences, Paddy. You know that."

"Don't call me that," Patrick said for the third time. "I know you're right, but still. I can't expect it to just *find* me.

"No, of course not. Unfortunately, I don't think I can help you with that. Maybe I can find someone who can. It'll take a couple of days. Hopefully your rabisu won't strike again before that." Liv got up and started to put the box back where it belonged. "That's all I can do for you now."

"There's something I don't understand," Julie interjected. "Why can Patrick catch this thing and not me? And why would the rabisu be drawn to him to begin with?"

"There are more things in heaven and earth, Horatio, than are dreamt of in your philosophy," Patrick answered with a hint of a smile.

Julie wasn't sure if he was making fun of her or not. She glanced at Liv, who glared at him. "You haven't told her, Patrick?"

"Of course not. I only just told Nataliya."

"Nataliya? Is that your girlfriend?"

"She's not my girlfriend," Patrick replied. "And I don't tell everyone my business. You only know because you found me."

"So you're not going to tell me, or what?" Julie asked.

Patrick looked at her and shrugged. "I don't know," he said. "Probably, but I don't feel ready now."

"I kind of want to be offended, but I don't have the energy. I want to find this thing. I have contacts too," Julie said.

"I don't doubt that the federal government has exhaustive resources. My contacts fly very much under the radar," Liv said.

Julie couldn't help but take it as a challenge. "Oh, really? Please. I know way more than you'd like to believe. And although I don't necessarily condone it, the government has a disgusting amount of information on these types of sources. I could probably find your contacts as well."

Liv just smiled. "Sure."

It rankled her more that Liv didn't try to argue. Perhaps she did know more than Julie. It made her uncomfortable. Unaware of Patrick's secret, she was definitely the least informed in the group. She didn't have extensive historical knowledge. She wasn't used to being in such a lower position.

"So this Nataliya, is she pretty?" Liv directed her question at Patrick. Julie was gratified to see that the man actually blushed. At least Julie wasn't being grilled about her love life.

"What does that have to do with anything?"

"I just never expected you to be this close to romancing someone. You always gave off a repressed vibe."

"Thanks a lot," Patrick mumbled.

"No, go with it!" Liv urged. She came back to sit at the table. "This red-haired Nataliya will melt your guarded, icy heart!"

"My heart is not icy."

"I suppose not. You always did have compassion. Hey, if you stick around, Martin will be home for lunch."

"Sorry, Liv, we have a lot of work to do on the case. I'll have to meet up with Martin another time. Give him my regards." Patrick stood up, and Julie followed suit. "It has been too long."

"Oh, wait." Liv leaned forward and plucked two sprigs of verbena from the potted plant. She gave one to each of them. "Verbena, or vervain, for protection. Keep it in your pocket."

"Thanks, Liv. For everything," Patrick said. He hugged Liv, and she returned it.

"Of course, Paddy."

"Don't call me that."

Ignoring him, Liv turned to look at Julie. "It was very nice to meet you, Agent Lyons. I hope we can stay in touch. I'm sure we can be of great help to each other in the future." She stuck out her hand.

Julie shook it, feeling a bit better about their earlier hiccup. "It was truly a pleasure, Ms. Masters."

"I'll walk you out."

The two followed the tiny woman, and Julie couldn't help but wonder if the verbena flowers in her pocket really would protect her. She much preferred her Glock.

CHAPTER SIXTEEN

Nataliya was startled awake by the sound of the morgue door slamming shut. She'd been working hard since Christmas, trying to find out as much as she could from the four bodies, and her sleep suffered from it.

"I told you to go home, Natashenka." Patrick sat down on the couch right by her knees. He leaned over and brushed a strand of hair from her eyes. "I don't want you to work yourself too hard."

Nataliya shrugged, though since she was lying on her side only one shoulder moved. "Are you only telling this to me because I'm pregnant?" she asked.

"Yes." Patrick's eyes sparkled with amusement. "You went to medical school and you were an intern. You know how to function with little sleep. But things are different now."

"Yeah. Not only am I going to push out a kid in a few months, but monsters are real." She sat up, feeling her vertebrae pop with the effort. The couch wasn't the most comfortable thing in the world, and her back complained. She could only imagine how much worse it would be when she started showing. "I didn't want to go home yet. I was waiting for you to get back. Where were you anyway?"

Patrick looked away, and it was his turn to shrug. "Seeing someone. An old friend. Well, sort of." He chuckled.

"What?"

"Nothing. I just know someone who deals with strange relics and is a religious historian. I wanted her advice on the rabisu and how to find it. She gave me a lot to think about. Julie went with me. I figured she might benefit from another contact."

"Oh, that's cool." Nataliya rubbed her eyes. She glanced at the clock and cringed. She'd slept for over two hours, which was way longer than she meant to. "I should go finish the paperwork."

"That can wait for Monday."

"No, it's fine. I should have gotten it done."

"As your boss, I'm telling you to leave it for Monday." Patrick smiled, but his tone was definitely stern. "Don't make me micromanage your life."

"Jeez, pulling the boss card on me?" Nataliya laughed. "God forbid I do something actually bad."

"I doubt that will ever happen. So far you've gone above and beyond what I expected of you from when we first met."

Nataliya gave him a sidelong glance. "And that's not just because you like me?" she asked.

"Of course not. That's separate." Patrick's expression turned serious. "I would never lie about professional matters. Or personal, for that matter. But what I feel for you does not affect how I view your work. I can't wait to see where you're going to go."

"Yeah, with a kid." She rubbed her forehead. "Not exactly how I imagined how this fellowship would go."

"Are you upset about it? I mean, you're allowed to feel however you want."

"It's not that I'm upset. I always wanted kids, especially while I was dating Alex. But the timing is so off." Nataliya didn't want to tell him everything she felt about her life. She was sure that the lines between personal and professional were completely gone now. But she didn't want to unload everything onto someone who was technically her boss.

"If there's one thing I've learned in my years on this earth, things don't always happen when we want them to. It's the curse of living with billions of other people who have their own lives and desires." Patrick sighed. "And when the unexpected happens, it can change everything."

"What happened that changed your life, then?" Nataliya asked. He looked down at his hands, and she knew she'd guessed right. He spoke from a painful experience.

"I haven't had a normal life, as I told you. When I realized the full scope of my abilities, my first guardian really didn't understand. He tried so hard to purge what he thought was bad out of me. When I left, I didn't expect things to turn out the way they did."

"What do you mean? Did he abuse you?"

Patrick shrugged again, which didn't answer her question. So she asked another. "But you are a medical examiner, and a highly respected coroner. You're pretty normal if you're just looking at you."

He looked up to meet her gaze. "I've always known what I am. The death of someone who is close to you is devastating enough when you're a normal person. But when you're me, and you can sense death, and the cause, and the time, and you can feel the soul being ripped from the body, sometimes in a violent matter, that death can feel like the universe is collapsing in your chest. I can see the souls of those who passed. They're not ghosts. They can't move or speak, but they can watch the living. They see me, and they know exactly who I am. That's why I wanted to be a medical examiner. I just didn't realize that losing someone close to me would change how I view death."

"Who died?" she asked.

He closed his eyes. She reached up to touch his cheek and he flinched. She was surprised, Patrick seemed to enjoy touching her when they were dancing, and when they spent Christmas Eve together.

"Is that why you've never let yourself get close to people? Is that why you never fell in love before me?"

"I'm sorry, you didn't need to hear me complain when I was supposed to be comforting you," Patrick said, forcing a smile. He looked away for a moment.

"I don't mind," Nataliya said. She was sincere. He turned once more to face her, and she noticed then how close they were. He seemed to lean forward slightly, as if to kiss her. He straightened up with a jolt.

"You should go home and get some real rest," he said, his tone completely different. "There's not much we can do now with no other cases and while I wait for Liv to get back to me with someone I can talk to about the rabisu."

"Are you sure?" Nataliya asked.

"Of course."

"You'd better tell me more later. I want to know."

"I know." Patrick smiled, but it looked strained. She remembered what he said in the alley on Christmas Eve. He'd hugged her tightly, and told her he wouldn't let her come to his rescue again. Suddenly, she realized that he'd been completely honest. It would destroy him if she got hurt. She said goodbye and got ready to leave. If Patrick was afraid of losing her, what would he do? He wouldn't be so cruel to push her away, would he? She was still sorting out her feelings for him, but she wanted to love him. She wanted to be with him. And he was scared in ways he couldn't vocalize.

Had it only been a few days since the world had been simple?

Beck woke up with a splitting headache. He'd gotten way too drunk again the night before, but at least he remembered everything. He groaned and rolled over. He sat up straight when he realized the other half of his bed was empty, then growled and flopped back down. She'd left?

He rubbed at his face, wondering if it was worth it to shower or not. He had the day off, thank all that was holy, and he felt like lying in bed like some gentleman of leisure who had nothing to do but sleep with pretty ladies and drink coffee.

But he didn't have servants, so he had to get up either way to get the damn coffee. Which he did begrudgingly. He pulled on a pair of boxers and wandered into the bathroom. It had been used recently, which meant that she'd showered before she left. Beck didn't know how to feel about that. He splashed his face with water and fought the urge to vomit before downing a couple of aspirin and drinking from the faucet. Elise had always hated when he did that, and she kept telling him to put a cup in the bathroom. If it had bothered her that much, she could have put the damn cup in there herself.

He wandered into the kitchen and measured out the coffee, feeling like his head was going to split open. Deciding that further hydration was a wise idea, he gulped down a glass of water and slumped into a chair. His mother had left him a vicious voicemail the night before, berating him for abandoning the family on Christmas Day. It wasn't anything new, but it still hurt to hear her disappointment.

Beck found his phone where he'd left it the night before, on the table, with barely any charge left. As the coffee brewed, he got up to get his charger and was shocked to see he had three missed calls, one from Julie, one from Patrick, and one from Harper. He cringed as he looked at the time stamps. Harper had called him at 7:00 AM. So that must have been around when she left his house. So why hadn't she awakened him instead? He groaned and listened to the voicemails Julie and Patrick left. Nothing much, just some more information on the victims of the family annihilator. Harper hadn't left a message. She probably had to get to work. He already regretted the fact that they slept together, but it had seemed like a good idea at the time.

He pushed that all aside and called Julie.

"It's about time that you joined the land of the living," she said instead of a normal greeting.

"I should have saved that level of drinking for the New Year's Eve party tomorrow."

"Beck, I don't care. There's been another mysterious death, outside of the city. Again. I'm going to check it out, but I can't invite you guys since it's in Illinois."

"Illinois again?" He shouldn't have been surprised with how close it was. "Where?"

"East St. Louis," she replied.

"Oh. Well." He didn't need to say much more. Though if this person was dead with no marks, it was highly unlikely to be gang related.

"Don't worry, I'll keep you informed. What are you doing for New Year's Eve?"

"I thought you didn't care," Beck snapped.

"I very quickly changed my mind. Whatever you're doing, I'm coming with you before you do something stupid like sleep with a coworker. Again."

Beck let out a laugh that sounded strained even to his ears.

"Jesus Christ, Beck. Goodbye." She hung up and he couldn't quite blame her for her irritation. Why she even bothered was beyond him. He didn't really appeal to others. He checked his work email and felt his heart sink when he saw that Mr. Randolph, the father-in-law of Brian Peralta, had suffered a fatal heart attack, most likely from the stress of losing his only daughter and only grandkids. It seemed so unfair.

"What the hell is going on?" Beck thought aloud. He had a feeling that Patrick was keeping something from him in regard to the cause of death, so he called Nataliya.

"Hello?" Nataliya sounded confused, which was to be expected. The last time they'd spoken alone had been awkward, to say the least.

"What aren't you two telling me about these murders?" he asked.

"I don't know what you're talking about."

"You're a very good liar, Nataliya. Now quit it. I know something weird is going on. Eight people don't just die like this. Eight young people with their hearts crushed?"

"I don't know, Beck. I really don't."

Beck frowned. He got up to get himself a cup of coffee. "There's something unnatural about all of this. I became a homicide detective because I wanted to solve murders. When I read your report on the

Peralta family, I didn't quite understand. After all, we caught the rapist killing women, right? Don't say it's a coincidence. It's not. There's absolutely no connection between the rapist and Brian Peralta. The only thing that's the same is the cause of death of all the victims, except the youngest son. That's bizarre."

"Beck, I don't know what to tell you. You should be having this conversation with Patrick."

"He won't tell me."

"Did you even try?"

Beck sighed and took a long drink of coffee. "Do you think he'd tell me, Talya?"

"Probably not. Maybe talk to Julie then," she suggested.

"I just did. She said there was another mysterious death in East St. Louis. Of course, no details."

There was a long silence, then, "Look, I have to go to a doctor's appointment. I'm sorry I can't tell you anything more, but it's not because I don't want to. We'll talk later. I really do have to run."

"I'm sorry," Beck said. "It's bad form to harass a pregnant woman, I guess. Not that I should have done it even if you weren't pregnant. I don't like feeling helpless."

"I understand. You've been through a lot. I hope you feel better soon."

"Thanks, Nataliya. You're a lot better of a person than I am. Good luck at the doctor." They hung up after saying goodbyes and Beck let out another sigh. He hated this. It wasn't just the feeling of helplessness. It was the fact that these people were purposefully keeping something from him. Regardless of their reasons, it felt almost deliberate. The worst part was he wasn't even sure if he blamed them. He was good at his job, but it was quite clear that he wasn't reliable. Too much alcohol, too many on- night stands, and not enough dealing with his pain in a healthy way.

He rubbed his face, wondering how the hell he was going to change his life when he didn't want to.

CHAPTER SEVENTEEN

Thirty-three years and never once had he thought he'd be in this position. Falling desperately in love with a woman. Patrick fiddled with the talisman that Liv had given him as she drove the two of them south and out of the city.

"What's with you?" Liv asked. "You're fidgeting."

"I just can't switch my brain off, I guess."

Liv gave him a sidelong look. "C'mon, Patrick, you're always steady as a stone. What's so different now?"

"I have stakes now," he said. "I've always known that everyone dies. But not knowing when others will die?"

"I'm sorry," Liv said. She sounded sincere. "I forget that you're not like the rest of us. And I mean that in a good way, Patrick."

Liv was sincere. She didn't call him Paddy. "I don't think I could go through losing someone again, Liv. It nearly destroyed me the first time." He didn't talk about this, ever, but he found he could tell Liv. She didn't really know any of his work colleagues, and she had sought him out to begin with. Even though she was thoroughly human, she seemed to understand a lot more than he might have guessed.

"I don't know anything about your relationship, but really. It's up to you," she said, keeping her eyes on the road.

"I can't just push her away. She's my fellow. She's supposed to be learning from me how to be a better medical examiner. She doesn't want to go to another coroner for the rest of her fellowship, and that wasn't what she applied for anyway. I can't help but feel like I ruined everything for her."

"Don't give yourself so much credit. She has as much choice in this as you do. But the fact is, you're confusing yourself. Love shouldn't be that difficult."

"Easy for you to say, you married the nicest man in the world who also happens to be extremely rich." Patrick shook his head. "Not everyone gets so lucky. Hell, Beck's wife cheated on him twice."

Liv chuckled. "You do have a point, but you also don't. What do you want? Without overthinking it, without thinking about the problems, what do you want?"

"Her."

"Yes. Good. Now why can't you have her?"

"Because I'm dangerous to love. She could get hurt if she tries to pursue anything with me. And if she is killed, it would destroy me. There's no choice that isn't selfish, I suppose." He looked out the window at the farmland. "She has as much choice in this as I do, as you said. I know she's attracted to me and that she likes me. She knows who I am, though I don't think she quite believes it. I'm coming to her with honesty. And she's not scared off."

"So you're going to suffer a broken heart either way." Liv studied him before turning back to the road. "Feeling her death would be the worse of the two, yes?"

"Yeah."

"Then there's your answer, if you're going strictly by pain. There's another factor you have to look at."

"And what's that?"

"If you pursue her, and she accepts it, the love is beyond anything else. Martin and I don't have the perfect marriage. We have our problems like anyone else. However, I wouldn't trade him for anything at all. I suppose that's easy considering our standard of living, but I can tell you that if I found out we lost everything, I'd still choose him. Every single day I choose him. Because I love him. I made a promise when we got married, and I'll keep it for as long as I live. I know his death won't affect me in the same way it would you, but I think I'd still choose Martin."

Patrick didn't reply. He carefully thought about what Liv was telling him.

"We're here." Liv pulled the car into a long driveway, tucked in between empty fields. She put the car in park and climbed out. Patrick followed, feeling awkward as she led the way. The house looked normal enough, just a farmhouse an hour and a half south of St. Louis. Liv rang the doorbell and stepped back to Patrick's side.

An old man answered, peering out with a scowl on his face. "What do you want?"

"I'm Liv Masters. I called you this morning?"

The man's scowl didn't disappear. "Who's that?" he said, tossing his head toward Patrick.

"The man I told you about. Dr. Patrick Morana."

The man turned to focus his glare on Patrick. He eyed him up and down, taking him in. "You don't look like much," he said.

"Neither do you," Patrick replied.

The man's eyes narrowed, but he opened the door wider. "Come in."

Liv, once again, led the way. She looked remarkably calm in the face of an old man who looked as if he'd chase them off his property with a sawn-off shotgun.

The house's interior didn't look much different from any older person's house. Photographs were on every wall, along with old wallpaper and old-fashioned linoleum flooring. The old man pointed at the couch, and Liv sat down with perfect posture. Patrick sat down next to her.

"So you're the one looking for the rabisu. I've been keeping up with the news. Didn't think that thing would have caused it, but they didn't say everything in the news reports." The man sat himself down on a recliner across from them.

"Criminal investigations often keep details out of the press," Patrick explained. "Sometimes it helps catch a murderer if they let slip details he couldn't have known unless he did the crime."

The man let out a grunt. "You work for the police?"

"I'm a medical examiner in St. Louis County." Patrick wasn't sure what the old man was getting at, but his scowl seemed to dissipate somewhat.

"You do work with the dead. I thought you might be a funeral director, though why one would need an MD I don't know." The man leaned back in the chair. "There's lots of things these murders could be. You sure it's a rabisu?"

"It was attached to his shoulders," Patrick said. "And I could feel it. I know these things."

The man grunted again, but he seemed satisfied. "I see you're wearing a talisman of obscurity. Did Liv get that for you?"

"Yes," she answered. "We've traded with you, just through a middleman. I've had my hands on many strange things."

The man didn't seem interested in her business as he kept his attention on Patrick. "You know that only those who have a true connection with Death can be safe from a rabisu, right? Even with an Obscuring, it can harm you."

"It won't kill me," Patrick said. That didn't mean it couldn't hurt him. "The Obscuring is to hide my connection."

The man rubbed his beard, looking thoughtful. His scowl had completely disappeared. "I think I can help you, then. I thought all the rabisu were gone by the fourteenth century. One reappearing here, in Missouri of all places, is bizarre." The man pointed at the mantel above the fireplace. "Purple hair, go get that basket up there.'

Liv smirked but she got up and retrieved the large basket. She had to go up on her tiptoes to do it. She brought it over to the man, who pulled a piece of cloth from the top. He rifled through it before coming up with a leather folio. He put the basket beside his feet and held the folio out to Patrick. "Here, sonny."

Patrick took it. It looked like a paintbrush case, but the objects inside were definitely not paintbrushes. He untied the straps and unrolled the folio. Inside the pockets were long rods, carved from a dark, hard wood. "What are these?"

"Similar to dowsing rods," the man said.

Patrick looked at the seven rods, wondering what the man meant. He'd seen modern dowsing rods, and they were L-shaped. These were all straight, about ten inches long. "These are supposed to help me find the rabisu?"

"Among other things. They're very old, older than Christianity anyway. All but one have a different design carved into it. Each rod corresponds with a different aspect of existence. You speak the Dead Tongue, yeah?"

"How'd you know that?" Patrick asked, very surprised.

The man chuckled. "You wouldn't be so blasé about chasing a rabisu if you weren't aligned with Death in some way, sonny. You admitted as much yourself. You'll be able to read the carvings then. You'll take the rod that has the aspect you're trying to find. It won't find human beings, which is rather unfortunate for demonic possession, but it will find altogether other creatures. Take the rod in your hand along with the blank rod in your other hand. They will start vibrating off each other in front of you. The harder the vibrations, the closer you are to the thing you seek. It's not a precise science, but as I said, more accurate than dowsing."

"Thank you." Patrick closed up the folio. "What do you want in return for these?"

The man scratched his beard. "Those are priceless. No amount of money in the world can replace those. The method of their creation is lost to history now. Not even purple hair over there would be able to find who made them and where the wood came from. So there's nothing you could give me."

"Can I borrow them then?" Patrick asked, feeling a sense of unease.

"You misunderstand me, sonny. I'm giving them to you."

"Why? I don't deserve such a gift."

The man let out a bark of laughter. "You are disgustingly humble. I know you're not a normal man. Think of it as returning a favor."

"But I don't even know you," Patrick said, his fingers tightening around the folio.

The man shrugged. "Nah, but I owe someone a favor I could never repay. Maybe those rods will be a start. Someday this will all make sense."

Patrick looked down and ran his fingers over the tooled leather. The case was obviously much newer than the rods. "I don't even know your name."

"It's not important. Now, get outta here. *Wheel of Fortune* is almost on. See yourselves out." The man waved them off, and Liv jumped to her feet. She grabbed Patrick's sleeve and tugged him toward the front door.

"Thanks. See you round," she said as they walked by.

"No, you won't," the man called out.

When they were back in the car, Patrick opened the folio again and pulled out one of the rods. The carvings were deep in the wood, and though the rods were smooth, the carvings weren't worn down. "This says *death*." He put the rod back and pulled out another one. "This says *urge*. This is what we'd use for the rabisu." He ran his fingers along the wood. "Liv, this wood."

"What?"

"I think I've seen it before. I don't know. It's probably just some ancient, extinct tree. Never mind."

Liv shook her head and started the car. "I hope they actually work."

"They do," Patrick said.

"How can you be sure?"

Patrick put the rod back in the case and ran his fingers over the seven rods. "These are old magic. At first I thought that the murders were being done by black magic, but it was done by an old forgotten monster. These rods were created to combat monsters of the ancient world. Magic nowadays has evolved from those methods of banishing evil. There's a reason the Judeo-Christian biblical texts denounced magic, more than just violating the supremacy of the power of Yahweh. The Qur'an forbids the practice as well, for the same reasons. Magic is like all kinds of power whether it be political, physical, religious. It can be twisted to evil without much effort."

"Yes." Liv put the car in gear and started driving back to the city. "The pursuit of power often conflicted with the worshiping of God as the highest and only source of power in the universe."

Patrick didn't exactly ascribe to all of Liv's religious beliefs, but he understood what she meant. He folded up the folio and tied it. "I think I may have been right after all. The rabisu wasn't just lying in wait for nearly a thousand years before returning. Something brought it back. Black magic."

Liv didn't seem to know what to say, so they both fell silent. She turned on the radio. Patrick had a feeling his troubles were only just beginning.

After Liv dropped him off at his house, he started readying for a prowl of the city. If he wanted to use the rods, he'd need someone to drive around the city with him. The logical choice was Julie, but she was going to a party for New Year's Eve that night. Of course, Beck would be there too. He could ask Julie anyway, because they had hours before the party started. Liv wouldn't have done it even if he had asked, and he couldn't put Nataliya in danger. If she hadn't been pregnant, he might have, but it seemed too risky. The rabisu would seize on any form of weakness. Patrick wouldn't have asked Beck either, even if the man had been aware of the seedy underbelly of the natural world. Beck was wrestling with alcohol, a divorce, and several other deep-rooted insecurities. He would be a far sight worse than Nataliya if they pursued the rabisu that preyed on sinful urges. Nataliya's weakness wasn't sin, just that growing a baby was a lot of work. And even though she wanted the child, it didn't change the fact that she was still wrestling with morning sickness, smell sensitivity, and exhaustion.

Patrick felt like an ass for thinking of her as weak. He didn't know one way or another. But he didn't want to put her at risk. His short list of people he could possibly ask was exhausted. He sat down on his chair in his little home office, the one where he'd made his healing potion. He felt a headache coming on from stress and lack of sleep. New Year's Eve. He had been invited to the party, but he'd said no, too intent on trying to find the rabisu before it struck again. The body in East St. Louis had been a normal heart attack with no evidence at all that it could have been the rabisu. So he had no idea where to even begin to look.

He checked his phone messages, which he hadn't done at all since Liv had picked him up to go visit the old man. Nataliya had texted him.

I'm going to that New Year's Eve party. Beck invited me. Are you coming? I need someone else sober there to keep me company.

He rubbed his fingers over his lips as he reread her message. Julie was going to be sober, as well. Surely Nataliya knew that. Patrick got up and went to his shelves, as if they held the answers to his dilemma. He had no choice but to ask Julie to help him. She had wanted to do it herself, in any case. She was an FBI agent. He was just a medical examiner. He texted her.

I need to find the rabisu. I may have a way of tracking it down. Can you help?

He looked at his watch. It was only 4:00 PM, and the party wasn't starting until 8:00 PM. While he waited for his response, he picked a book from one of the top shelves and pulled it down. There was no title on the book, just an embossed leather cover. It was old, as old as some of Liv's books. The words were hand-inked, but it had no illuminations and no illustrations. He rifled through pages until he found what he was looking for.

To Cast Out a Creature of the Darkness

He picked at his lip as he read the incantation. It was in the Dead Tongue. He didn't need outside verification to know if it would work. The very fact that it was written in the Dead Tongue was its verification. He took a photo of it with his phone, as the book was too unwieldy to carry with him. He then double checked that the talisman of obscurity that Liv gave him was around his neck. The vervain was in his pocket, as it had been since she'd given it to him a couple of days before. He took up the leather folio and sat down to really look at each of the rods.

Death

Urge

Wrath

Destruction

Pestilence

Wasting

He didn't know if he would have chosen such aspects of the dark world. Two were Horseman, and some were in common with the Seven Deadly Sins. But he wasn't the ancient magic worker who had carved them. His fingers ran along the carvings for Death. It had a tingle of power that pulled at him, calling his baser nature. It was him. He was Verum Mortem. He hadn't told Julie exactly what that meant, though she'd asked. True Death. His Father was the personification of Death. Patrick had inherited the understanding and affinity for the concept. The divining rod, as he chose to call it, had been imbued with some sort of stuff that could recognize who he was.

Patrick took hold of the blank rod and held it in his other hand. There was a slight buzzing. He wondered why it wasn't stronger, before he remembered he wore the talisman. He took it off, and this time when he held the rods they vibrated so violently that it hurt his hands. He nearly dropped them before he let them fall to the floor. They bounced off the carpet, unharmed. Patrick put the talisman back on and was relieved that the rods only held a slight buzz. He wouldn't be able to use the rods without the masking of his person. He had to figure out how to get a talisman for himself. He couldn't pay money, but maybe he could find another way to repay Liv.

His text notification went off, so he packed up the rods and checked Julie's response.

Sure. I'll have Nataliya keep an eye on Beck at the party. I'd much rather hunt down a creature of evil than babysit the dumbass.

The last thing Nataliya deserved was that task, especially since she couldn't drink and probably didn't care too much about Beck's foibles. It was the only choice he had, though, so he arranged for Julie to pick him up at his house. He went to change clothes. He needed warmer layers in case he had to get out of the car to follow a lead.

He sat on his front stoop to wait for Julie. He didn't wear gloves, which he figured would affect his sensitivity toward the rods. He tapped his fingers on his knees, feeling that they were wasting time they didn't have.

CHAPTER EIGHTEEN

Four hours of prowling the city and surrounding suburbs produced nothing. The only positive aspect to the experience was that Julie finally had an intimate understanding of the road systems of St. Louis, and Patrick had explained the various pronunciations of each of the roads. No wonder everyone had given her a weird look when she said Gravois. She'd only pronounced it as her GPS had, "Grav-wah." Nope, it was "Grav-oy." Leave it to Americans to massacre French words.

After the disappointment of not finding the rabisu, Julie drove them to the party. She'd expected to miss it, but since it seemed the rabisu was lying low, they both decided to take a break and enjoy the night. Well, Julie decided. Patrick looked too deep in thought to even care.

"I just don't understand why I'm not getting anything. I would have thought I might have gotten something, even just an indication of where it was, but I only felt the same underlying buzz as before." Patrick looked at the rods in his hand. He'd given her a brief explanation on how they worked.

"Can I try?" she asked. She put the car in park a couple of blocks away from Officer Reynolds's apartment. Patrick handed over the rods. Sure enough, there was a slight buzz once she had both rods in her hands. "Wow. Can anyone use these?"

"I suppose so, as long as you understand what you seek and what the rods trace. If I gave it to Beck without an explanation I don't think he'd feel anything."

Julie handed the rods back. "Is it possible the rabisu fled the area?"

"Of course it's possible," Patrick said. He sounded dejected. "And if that's the case it could be anywhere."

"We've had no word on Brian Peralta," Julie said. "He didn't take his cell phone so we couldn't trace the signal, and though his truck was distinctive, we saw no sightings of it. His credit cards showed nothing. Essentially we're dead in the water until he kills again."

"Did you put out the word about the unusual CODs?"

"I did as soon as you told me about the Peralta family's CODs." Julie shook her head. "This is going to be like finding a needle in a haystack."

"It will kill again," Patrick said. "If Peralta had the urge to kill his own family, there's no telling what else it could make him do. I wish I knew more about it. To see if it hibernates at all. Or if it only jumps if the host dies or if it's pulled off."

"Why did it jump to begin with? And how did it hit Peralta?"

Patrick shrugged. Julie wondered if he was hiding something. He had an amazing poker face, but she was specially trained to read people. There was something he didn't want her to know. Julie hadn't known him too long, but her instincts told her that he wouldn't withhold anything that would hurt their chances of finding the rabisu. She hoped she wasn't wrong.

"Let's go in," she said. "Maybe we should sleep on it. I haven't found anything about rabisu from any of my contacts, anything other than what we found at Liv's."

"I'm not surprised." Patrick unbuckled his seatbelt, and the two of them got out of the car and walked toward Reynolds's house. It was well below freezing and pitch black between the streetlights. Julie shivered in her coat. Patrick didn't seem as bothered.

They got to Reynolds's house, which had a large yard. The entire house was lit up with Christmas lights, and they could hear music and laughter from inside.

"You okay?" Julie asked, realizing Patrick still didn't look all that present.

"I'm fine," he said. "I'm just not in the mood to party."

"You never seemed like the party type. Fancy weddings, sure, but drunken work parties, not so much."

Patrick managed a smirk. "You guessed right. I was the boring guy in my college dorm, studying all night when my roommates were off at frat parties and hooking up."

"Well, as someone who also went to frat parties, I think you had the better end of the deal." Julie chuckled. "I remember a particular incident with red licorice and vodka. I don't care to repeat that experiment. Ever."

They walked into the house to find a sea of cops. Most were out of uniform, and Julie had a bit of trouble recognizing the ones who weren't plainclothes detectives. She hadn't bothered much with memorizing everyone's names, which felt a bit elitist. But she was busy in the local FBI office. Patrick greeted a few people, who greeted him back. A couple recognized Julie, and she was grateful when she remembered them.

They found Beck and Nataliya on a couch in a sitting room by a roaring fireplace. Christmas decorations crowded out the mantelpiece, along with stockings. There were a few candles lit, despite the overhead lights, and Nataliya looked pained. Beck was half reclined on the couch, beer in hand.

Julie shot Patrick a look. He returned it with a roll of his eyes. They crossed the room and Nataliya's eyes lit up. "You made it!" she exclaimed. "Beck here is telling me all about Elise."

"Good god, already?" Julie looked at Beck. "How much have you had?"

"Just this." Beck tipped his beer bottle toward her. "But sometimes you just gotta get out your troubles, right?"

"To be fair, I asked." Nataliya let out an awkward giggle. She sidled over to Patrick and Julie. "Of all the times to have enforced abstinence from alcohol," she muttered, just quiet enough that Beck couldn't hear over the music.

Patrick patted her on the shoulder a bit awkwardly. "Do you want water or anything?"

Julie ignored them and walked over to sit down uncomfortably close to Beck. "You need to stop bitching about your ex to everyone," she said, her tone low and menacing

Beck jumped at the bite in her words and shrank away. "You're scary when you're angry," he said.

"Angry?" Julie smiled. "Who said I was angry?" She grabbed the bottle out of his hand. "You're drinking a big glass of water between beers, fuckboy."

"I'm not a fuckboy, Julie."

"That's not what Elly says." Julie took a swig of the beer and handed it back. Beck looked as if she'd spit in it.

"Elly can fuck right off. What the hell did you do that for?"

Julie shrugged. "Just showing you how uncomfortable I can make you, so maybe you can stop making other people uncomfortable by shutting the fuck up about Elise."

Beck's look of mortification was worth it. "I thought you had work to do. You came in with Patrick?"

"We were chasing a lead."

"You and Patrick? Why didn't you let me know?"

Julie shrugged. "He called me. Ask him if you're so curious. Besides, nothing came of it. And now they're going to go be teetotalers in the corner and talk about puppies and babies and shit."

"Do you have something against puppies and babies?" Beck asked.

"I mean, both are lovely. But as you well know, people in our line of work aren't exactly known for stable marriages. I could get reassigned anywhere in the US on a whim. And I work too long hours to properly take care of either. And that's fine with me." Julie somewhat envied Nataliya and Patrick, mostly because they had stable jobs that were usually not dangerous. Patrick sort of threw himself into danger, but it was hard not to when you were one of the few people who knew about the things that go bump in the night. As for Nataliya, she would make decent money, she was apparently on good terms with her ex, and she didn't have much to worry about in the grand scheme of things.

Julie missed the days of her ignorance. She would have given a lot to go back, long before she joined the FBI. But that wasn't going to happen.

"I would have made a shitty dad," Beck said.

"Probably," Julie agreed.

Beck sighed and Julie helped herself to a bottle of beer on the coffee table. She popped off the cap and clinked her bottle to Beck's. "Here's to the two of us not having kids because we'd be shitty at it."

"To us," Beck said. "I thought you were going to be my designated driver."

"We'll make Nataliya do it," Julie said. "It's been a long-ass week, and I am so over it."

"You and me both."

They drank their beers in silence.

Nataliya tapped on the steering wheel, feeling rather irritated as Patrick tried to load Julie and Beck into her car. The two were blistering drunk and spent the countdown to the New Year vomiting in Reynolds's backyard. She had half a mind to leave them to figure out their own transportation, but Patrick appealed to her sense of kindness. After all, it wouldn't do to leave a homicide detective and an FBI agent to their own devices where anyone could find them.

Patrick had specifically forbidden her from trying to wrangle either of them, due to her pregnancy and the fact that both of them smelled vaguely of vomit. Nataliya was a sympathetic vomiter these days, and she was tired of it. The problem wasn't that Beck and Julie were unruly, but that they were practically blackout drunk. Patrick had to manhandle Beck into the car. Beck wasn't a small man. And Julie's lean frame hid a muscular body. Finally, Patrick had them both in the back seat, belted up. He got into the passenger seat and let out a sigh.

"I'm so sorry, Nataliya," he said. "I had no idea Julie was going to drink so much. I guess it doesn't matter now."

"It's fine." Nataliya started driving. She rolled down the windows just enough to air out the car. It was even colder now that it was well past midnight, but she'd rather shiver a bit than smell Beck and Julie. "Does Beck often do this?"

"Not like this," Patrick replied. "I haven't seen him this bad since he kicked out Elise in May. And I've never seen Julie remotely tipsy."

Nataliya was not impressed. She drove first to Julie's apartment, then to Beck's house. Patrick, again, had to wrangle each of them to get them safely inside. He came back to the car, looking more than a little grumpy. "Thank you for the ride," he said. "Julie and I went around the city looking for Brian Peralta and we came straight to the party."

"It's no trouble," she said with a smile. She was happy to roll the windows up and drive him home. He hadn't had any alcohol either, choosing to join her in abstinence. The party hadn't been very fun for her, but she was so tired these days and so often sick. She'd even lost weight, which the doctor had told her was totally normal.

The drive to Patrick's house was quiet. The radio played softly, a counterpoint to her intense thinking. She glanced at Patrick, but his face was hard to read in the dark interior of her car. She hadn't thought about how much her life would change come late July. She knew in an abstract way that nothing would be the same again, but the enormity of that change had been pushed to the side as she steeled herself to reveal the pregnancy to her parents and solve murder cases. Patrick's confession to her on Christmas Eve only complicated matters. He didn't seem concerned with explaining further, though he hadn't indicated that questions were unwelcome. She didn't know what to think, but the more she researched the murders, the more she was inclined to believe in the supernatural. And she never could adequately explain what she saw in the alley. The rabisu.

"What is that necklace?" she asked.

Patrick raised his hand to clasp the glass bauble. "It's a talisman of obscurity. Or deceit, depending on your point of view. It hides my nonhuman nature. That's the only way I can confront the rabisu."

"Oh," Nataliya replied as if she understood. She didn't, but she wasn't sure if she wanted to ask more.

"I'm one of the very few people who can stop it. Julie and I prowled all over the city and we didn't find anything. We're worried it moved on."

"That's awful," Nataliya said. "I hope you can find it.'

"Yeah. Me too." He fell silent and she went back to concentrating on the road. Shaw neighborhood wasn't far from Beck's house.

"I don't think I'm as scared as I should be," she said finally. "You told me black magic is real and that your father is the Grim Reaper."

"Technically he's—"

"I'm being hyperbolic," she interrupted. "And anyway, it's just hard to take in, you know? With everything else going on in my life, I can't help but accept all this dark stuff as a matter of course. Of course my boss would be the son of death. Of course I'd get pregnant by accident. Of course you'd be chasing an ancient demonic force around St. Louis. Of course Beck would get blackout drunk on New Year's Eve." She shook her head. "The only good thing is the baby." She let out a chuckle. "Oh man, my roommate is going to be pissed."

"How come?"

"Nurse's hours and babies don't mix. I guess I'll have to find a new place to live. There's no way in hell I'd move in with Alex. I'm making more money at the morgue, though. It won't be as hard to find a new apartment and pay off my student loans. Having a baby is going to complicate that regardless."

"I guess I never thought of that," he said. "Obviously I never really had to."

Nataliya pulled up behind Patrick's car in front of his house. "Lucky you. I always figured this situation would happen in a two-income family." She shrugged. "But I'm luckier than most. I have a great job and supportive parents. Or they will be supportive when I tell them."

"You haven't told them yet?"

She let out a chuckle. "No. Mama is going to want to fly out immediately, and I am not prepared for that. I almost want to wait until after the rabisu is caught, but who knows when that will be? Anyway, I'll probably tell them in a week or so."

Patrick nodded. "It's good that your parents love you that much."

"I know. I really do miss them. I may complain about them, but I don't know what I'd do without them. They've done nothing but support me. They didn't even care about my career choice. They thought it was important. They came from a place where people would go missing and no one cared about where they want. People would die and no one would look into their deaths. They think that becoming a medical examiner is very important. And I don't think they'll be very thrilled with me getting pregnant by my ex, but they won't make a big deal about it. Besides, they've always wanted grandchildren to spoil." She chuckled. "And it's not like I'm a sixteen-year-old girl in high school. They're going to love the kid to death. He or she is going to have everything they ever wanted."

"She's lucky," Patrick said.

"She? You kind of implied the baby was a girl before."

"I'm not implying it. I'm telling you." He gave a one-shoulder shrug. "But you don't have to take my word for it. Thank you again for the ride. I'd ask you to come in for tea or something, but I know you're exhausted. I'll talk to you tomorrow." He got out of the car and waved before climbing up the steps to the front door. Nataliya watched him walk away, feeling something akin to amusement. She wasn't sure whether to believe him about the baby, but he'd known she was pregnant before she did.

Patrick stumbled and tumbled down the stairs. Nataliya gasped and lunged toward the door, the seatbelt trapping her. A shadow separated from the darkness and pounced on top of Patrick and shoved his head into the concrete path. Even in the darkness, she could see the shadow had solid form. She unbuckled her seat belt and launched herself out of the car. Patrick was groaning in pain and the shadow moved an arm forward until it gripped his throat.

"Stop. Looking. For. Me," it said, the voice gravelly.

"Get off him!" Nataliya stayed behind the front of the car. She had her phone in one hand and she reached into the pocket of her coat. "I'm going to call 911."

"For what?" The shadow rose and a mere sliver of moonlight fell across its face. It was a man, and she recognized him from the photo that had been passed around. Brian Peralta. "This thing is useless." Brian grabbed Patrick's necklace and ripped it off his neck. Patrick groaned again, and Nataliya saw a dark wetness on the side of his face. He was bleeding.

Nataliya withdrew her phone and started dialing. Brian leaped off Patrick and tackled her in a blink of an eye. She screamed, and her phone slipped out of her hand. Brian didn't bother with her anymore, and instead he stomped on the phone, crushing it to bits.

"Stop looking for me, Son of Death," Brian shouted. "I can't kill you, but I can kill her." He pointed at Nataliya. "If you look for me again, I will rip the child from her and strangle her with her own hair." He took off running into the night.

Patrick staggered to his feet, one hand clutching at the side of his head. "Natashenka. Nataliya?"

"I'm fine," she said, putting her hands up. "I landed in the grass." Patrick didn't have a big yard, but there was just enough ground to have a lawn. The ground was cold and hard, but she didn't fall on the concrete pathway. "You have a head wound."

"You need to leave."

The sound of people opening their front doors barely reached her. The shouts and her scream had alerted Patrick's neighbors.

"Not right now, I have to look at that. Even if you can heal fast, you could have more damage." Nataliya got to her feet, much more easily than Patrick. She was being honest when she said she wasn't hurt. It was more of a jolt than anything, and she didn't even think she'd be bruised. Brian wasn't trying to hurt her, just stop her from calling 911. She took Patrick's arm and led him into his house. She had to unlock the door for him as he was spacey from the head wound.

"You can't stay here. He's going to kill you."

"He said only if you continue looking for him. And you're in no shape to do that tonight, Patrick."

She led him into the kitchen and made him sit down on the chair. She turned on the lights and he squinted against the brightness. He looked at his hand, covered in blood. "What? I mean, he could be lying. He could come kill you."

"That's a risk I'm going to take." Nataliya rummaged around in his drawers until she found a towel. She put some water on to boil and began wiping the blood from his neck and face. He had struck the side of his head on the concrete stairs, and it appeared the wound was a couple of inches above his ear. It was a lot nastier than she was prepared for. "How hard did he hit you?"

Patrick blinked a few times. She tilted his chin up to look in his eyes. She didn't have a penlight, but even in the kitchen lighting she could see his pupils were dilated.

"Patrick, you need to go to the hospital and get X-rays. You have a concussion or worse."

"What?" He squinted against the lights again. "No, I don't want to get x-rays. I can't let them examine me."

"Can you heal a brain injury as fast as a burn?"

"What burn?"

He was definitely confused. He had some sort of brain injury. While she could suture him up here in the kitchen, if he had other problems she didn't have the equipment to help him in his house. She didn't know how to make healing potions, at least not magical ones. "He broke my phone," she said. "Come on, I'm going to take you to the hospital."

He shook his head, then grimaced as the action caused him further pain. "No, they can't see me."

"I'm not arguing with you. Come on." She took his arm and tugged him out of the chair. He moved to stand up, but it was clear he was having balance issues, so she let him sit back down. She tried to remember what she'd seen when Brian pounced on him. Maybe he had forcibly slammed Patrick's head onto the concrete step on purpose. That could cause a more serious injury than an accidental fall, perhaps.

She let Patrick sit back down. "Stay still for me, okay?"

He didn't protest when she pulled his phone out of his pocket. She unlocked it, halfway hoping that Patrick wouldn't remember she knew his passcode, and dialed a number still bright in her mind.

"Wingate," a familiar male voice said.

"It's me," she said.

"I'd assume this was a drunk call, but you're pregnant." His tone was amused.

"Alex, have you been drinking at all tonight? Or are you on shift?"

"I'm on shift," Alex said, his entire demeanor changing when he heard her urgency. "What's wrong?"

"Dr. Morana has a head injury. He's pretty reluctant to go to the hospital, and I can't take care of him here. He's bleeding, confused, and his pupils are different sizes. If he has a concussion, I would never forgive myself for letting him stay here. He'd probably feel better about going if it was more on the downlow."

"Downlow? He works for the county. They're going to want to know if he can't perform his job, Nataliya."

"That's not exactly what I mean. I just want you to look him over. If he's not as bad as all that, we can go home and forget it ever happened. But if it's worse, then we can figure it out," she said.

"Okay, I get it. You don't want it to be official unless he needs to be admitted. Fine. I've done crazier things for you. Bring him in. New Year's is never boring. At least we haven't had a DUI accident tonight. Yet."

"Don't jinx yourself. Thank you so much, Alex, you have no idea how much this means to me."

"Yeah, I think I do." Alex's voice sounded wry, and she wasn't sure what he meant by that. "I'll see you in a few."

She hung up and turned to Patrick. He was looking up at her, clearly still spacey.

"You called your ex?" he asked.

"You heard what I said. If it's not bad, no report. We can talk about details when you're coherent."

Patrick rubbed at his eyes, smearing blood on his face. "Fine. I give up. Let's go." He tried to stand and swayed. She rushed over and grabbed his waist. "This is the second time you've helped me after a rabisu attack. Why is it always around parties?"

"Just lucky, I guess," Nataliya said. "Come on, I don't want to waste any more time."

CHAPTER NINETEEN

Nataliya sat in the padded chair, wringing her gloves in her hands. Patrick had gone back for X-rays, and of course they wouldn't let her back, even if she was a doctor. Not if she was pregnant. And she would just be in the way of the tech anyway. So she sat in the ER room that Alex had waiting for them. He'd had to pull a few strings, as the night had gotten very busy, as expected. She could hear someone in the next room vomiting, and she squeezed her gloves harder to fight the nausea that roiled in her belly.

She'd told Alex most of what had happened, leaving certain details out. She didn't think Patrick had lost consciousness, or if he had, it was for less than a minute or so. He had vomited on the car ride over, and Nataliya was glad she'd stashed plastic grocery bags when she first started getting morning sickness. It saved her from driving a puke smelling car for the next few weeks. Alex had ordered X-rays, and the nurse whisked him away. Now she was alone, waiting for the results. Patrick had been so disoriented and off-balance that they didn't even bother with a wheelchair. He was wheeled around on his hospital bed, hooked up to an IV. She'd worked enough brain injuries during her residency that she knew he was getting diuretics, anti-seizure meds, and a mild painkiller.

The nurse, a pretty Black woman in her late thirties returned after far too long. "I'm sorry to keep you waiting," she said.

Nataliya got to her feet, happy that someone had finally come to talk to her. "Can you tell me what's going on? X-rays don't take that long."

The nurse bit her lip. "Dr. Nataliya Vasilyeva, right?"

"Yes, that's me. What's going on?"

"Dr. Morana asked that we tell you what's happening. Well, he's in emergency surgery right now. Dr. Wingate found an intracranial hematoma. Subdural. Dr. Morana was close to slipping into a coma by the time the anesthesiologist came in." The nurse, whose name tag said Carrie, shook her head. "The cut on his temple was the least of his worries, really. But he's in the best hands in the city."

"Yeah, I know." Nataliya collapsed in the chair. "I've known Alex for a long time."

The nurse nodded, though she didn't comment. The person in the next room vomited again. "Dr. Morana will be in surgery for a while longer, and he's going to be in the hospital for a few days. You might be more comfortable in the waiting room, especially away from that."

"Thanks, Carrie," Nataliya said. "I'm just surprised he was coherent enough to give you permission to tell me his status."

"I think Alex might have had something to do with that. He said he was your boss and that you two were pretty close." Carrie shrugged.

That was weird, but Nataliya didn't say so. "Yeah. He doesn't have any family. I'm doing a fellowship under him as a medical examiner."

"Oh, so you're Alex's ex!" Carrie exclaimed with a laugh.

"Wait, he talked about me?"

"Yeah! He was so excited when he found out he was going to be a dad." Carrie chuckled again. "I told him being a parent can be hard, long nights, cranky colicky babies, but I don't think he really cares."

"Yeah, that sounds about right. I'd better let you get back to work."

"Oh, of course. Sorry. Do you know where the OR waiting room is?"

Nataliya nodded, and Carrie led her out into the ER hallway. "We'll come find you when Dr. Morana is out of surgery. It could take a while. I didn't see the X-rays, so I'm not sure how serious it is. But Alex seemed concerned."

"Thanks, Carrie."

Nataliya didn't go right to the waiting room. She wandered the hospital a bit, feeling a sense of déjà vu. It had been one week since Patrick had been in the hospital the last time. Only then his arms had been burned. Now he was in surgery with blood pooling on his brain.

She took a deep breath and headed toward the maternity ward. Carrie's thoughts on being a parent rang in her head. Her realization that her roommate wasn't going to be happy about having a baby around was still fresh in her mind, in spite of the rabisu attack. What was she going to do? Patrick was going to try and convince her to leave the fellowship, considering the fact that he'd been attacked twice in her presence. She'd barely been scuffed, but now the rabisu had threatened her life. And her baby's life. She shuddered as she remembered his words.

Before too long, she was in the maternity ward. Things were different from TV, and there wasn't a window she could use to look at the newborns. The babies were almost always kept in the mother's room now, unless there were complications. But wandering the halls, looking at the photos of babies who had gone through the NICU and come out none the worse, the baby art on the walls, and the people who seemed to be excited rather than worried, she felt some sense of fear. Patrick wasn't going to stop hunting this thing, Nataliya knew that much. He wouldn't put her in danger, but he had such a unique identity that she couldn't imagine him letting it go. Not after it threatened her.

"Were you looking for someone?"

Nataliya looked over at the nurse's aide. The young woman wasn't any older than twenty-one or so. She was pretty, with dark hair, dark eyes, and a knowing look.

"Uh, no," Nataliya said. "My boss is in surgery."

The aide looked perplexed for a brief moment, but the expression disappeared. "Let me know if you need anything."

Nataliya nodded, but got the hint. She didn't belong there. She left the ward and went back down to neurology and sat down in the OR waiting room. She tapped her fingers on her knees, feeling restless. She didn't have her phone and though she still had Patrick's, she didn't know who to call. Both Beck and Julie were trashed and wouldn't be of any use well into the next day. With nothing else to do, she curled up on the cushioned bench and fell asleep.

You are a damn fool.

"I know I am. You will never let me forget that."

You let that thing get the best of you. And it got away before you could destroy it. Has nothing I taught you remained in that human brain of yours?

"Sterling tried like hell to beat it out of me."

You are not ready to join your father. Not like this.

"You know how I die."

I have always known how you will die, and it will not be by such mundane means. The last time you breathe will not be the last time you will be awake.

"How do I die then, if a rabisu is mundane?"

It is not right for a man to know the time and means of his death, not even the Son of Thanatos. Wake now. And do not disappoint me again.

"Dr. Morana?"

Patrick opened his eyes and immediately shut them. The room wasn't very bright, but it was bright enough that the light sent a searing pain through his head. "Nngg?" he managed.

"You weren't speaking English just now."

Patrick licked at his lips. He opened his eyes again and looked at the nurse, though her features were blurry. "I guess not," he said.

The nurse let out a relieved sigh. "I'm glad to see you're awake." And coherent, Patrick added to himself.

"What's going on?" he asked. He tried to lift his hand, but an IV was taped firmly in place.

"Do you remember what happened last night?" the nurse asked.

"I remember driving home from a party with Nataliya."

The nurse nodded.

"Then nothing," he said. That wasn't true, but he didn't quite know how much to divulge. He wasn't thinking straight yet, and he didn't want to spill anything about the rabisu in this state when she was probably already wondering about his head injury and if he had brain damage.

"Okay. Let me check your vitals, and I'll call in Dr. Wingate."

Why did that name seem familiar?

The nurse took his vitals, wrote on his chart, and left. Patrick licked his lips again. He could kill for a drink. The last thing he did remember was the rabisu smashing his head into the concrete. His heart leaped into his throat. Nataliya! Where was she? Had it attacked her? Was she okay?

After a few more endless moments, the nurse returned with a familiar man. Patrick blinked, and then finally remembered him as Nataliya's ex-boyfriend Alex. Dr. Wingate.

"You're a lucky man," Alex said, moving to his bedside. "You got through surgery better than expected. It also helped that Nataliya called me so quickly after you were injured."

Patrick wasn't sure what to say. He just looked at the other man. They were about the same age, and he supposed he could understand why Nataliya had dated him. Getting past his success in his career, he was a handsome, well-built man with an easy smile. It was clear that Dr. Wingate smiled a lot more than Patrick did.

"Is Nataliya okay?" Patrick asked, feeling wretched that he had to even voice his fear.

"She's fine," Dr. Wingate said. "Just a bit shook up, though she didn't exactly tell me what happened." He shrugged. "You're going to heal up quick. You'll be out of here in no time."

Patrick moved his IV-free hand and rubbed his eyes. He didn't want to be here at all. "Thank you," he said finally. Recent memories started filtering back. Dr. Wingate had explained to him what they were going to do, and Patrick knew the man was relieved he didn't have to put it into layman's terms. One of the advantages of treating another doctor. Patrick hadn't looked forward to having holes drilled into his skull, but it was better than a craniotomy.

"You're welcome," Dr. Wingate said, his smile dissolving to something softer. Not a frown, but something Patrick couldn't read. "She really cares about you."

Patrick didn't know what to say to that. He licked his lips.

"As I said, you're a lucky man." This time Dr. Wingate's expression was very readable. Patrick didn't need a psychologist to explain to him that Dr. Wingate was still very much in love with Nataliya.

"Is she still here?" Patrick asked.

"Yep. I don't think she would have left this place if it were on fire, as long as you were still here. Thankfully the hematoma wasn't large, but it was at risk of pressing against your brain enough to create damage." Dr. Wingate switched easily into his professional demeanor. "You're going to need to take it easy for a while. Let the others take the lead on the autopsies. I don't want you lifting heavy weights or engaging in exercise for at least two weeks. We'll test your motor function before you leave, and then we can determine how long you need to abstain from driving. And speaking of abstaining, I'm prescribing you meds that you absolutely cannot mix with alcohol."

"Yeah, I figured. I'm not a big drinker in any case."

"Good." Dr. Wingate smiled again. "You know the recovery protocol, I suppose."

"Yes. Even though I've spent the last few years working on corpses, some things you don't forget."

"All right. It's almost sunrise. I should let you get as much rest as you can. I'll have the nurses fill you in on all the other details. But really, the surgery went remarkably well. I'm not just saying that."

Again, Patrick didn't know what to say. He did heal fast. But even he couldn't fix some things without intervention.

"I'll tell Nataliya she can come see you on my way out. But get some good, real rest," Dr. Wingate said as a final caution. "Brains are funny things, and too much excitement post-surgery can only end in tears." He let out a breath that was just the far side of a snort and left the room. Patrick rubbed his eyes again. Alex hadn't asked about how he'd gotten the injury. He wasn't sure if he was thankful or concerned. Either way, Nataliya wouldn't have given anything away.

A few moments later, Nataliya came into the room. She looked exhausted, and it was clear she hadn't slept at all while he'd been in surgery.

"*Bozhe!*" She hurried over and took his hand. "You scared me half to death, Patrick."

He couldn't help but chuckle at the expression. He lifted his other hand, the one with the IV, and touched her hair, then her cheek. "Not at all. I'm still here."

Without coaxing, Nataliya crawled into the hospital bed next to him. It looked as if she was about to cry. "I don't want to lose you," she whispered into his shoulder. She was tucked against him, small and trembling.

"That's my line," Patrick said, moving so that she could fit next to him more comfortably. Hospital beds weren't made to sleep two, even if one of them was a small woman. "After everything, you're still here."

"I wouldn't be anywhere else."

Alex Wingate's words echoed in his mind. He'd said she wouldn't have left Patrick's side if the hospital were on fire. Alex was still in love with Nataliya, but he knew that between the two of them, she'd chosen Patrick. He felt the warmth of her body next to his. Both times he'd been attacked, she'd been there. Both times, she'd been in danger, and both times, she hadn't thought about herself. He wanted to protect her, but he didn't know how.

And still, she'd chosen him. He couldn't help but fall hopelessly in love.

CHAPTER TWENTY

New Year's Day was overcast, and Julie was incredibly grateful. She nursed her bottle of water laced with vitamin C powder, and she had taken probably a few more aspirin than was healthy for her kidneys. She walked past Patrick's room without realizing it and had to be steered back by a judgmental nurse. Not that she could blame her; Julie was wearing her dark glasses inside, and instead of her usual fed suit, she wore gray sweats and a hoodie. And flip flops, in spite of the freezing weather. Laces just seemed too complicated with a splitting headache.

She knocked on the door to Patrick's room, and she heard him call to come in. She went in, taking another swig of water as she did so.

"Mornin'," she said. Patrick lay on the hospital bed in a gown, and he had a bandage on the side of his head, covering up part of his hair.

"It's 3:00 PM," Patrick said, pointing at the clock on the wall. "Good lord, Julie, between the two of us, you look worse, and I had emergency brain surgery last night."

"Pretty sure the Everclear did us in," Julie said. She collapsed on one of the chairs in the room. "I couldn't even wake up Beck."

Patrick scoffed. "How much did you drink, anyway?"

"No clue. We lost count at a number I'm not going to say." Julie pulled her sunglasses down just enough to try and get a good look at Patrick. The light was too harsh, so she pushed them back up her nose. "I took a rideshare here. What happened to you? Nataliya only said there was an accident. Probably because I wasn't very coherent on the phone."

"The rabisu," Patrick said. "It was waiting for us at my house, still attached to Brian Peralta."

"Jesus. What did it do?"

"It tackled me to the ground, and it slammed my head onto the concrete stairs to my front door. It threatened Nataliya and knocked

211

her down too. She wasn't hurt, though, she fell on the grass. It did break her phone."

"Oh. So that's why she called from yours." She hadn't connected the dots that Nataliya had called from Patrick's number. She'd half expected that they had to have hooked up, not that Patrick had been attacked. "How come you didn't notice it was there?"

"I wasn't using the dowsing rods, I guess. Not that it was much help when we searched the city yesterday."

"I'm surprised it didn't kill you when it had the chance." Julie sipped at her water, wishing for coffee. The acidity would only make her throw up again, and she was tired of heaving.

Patrick was silent for a long moment. It seemed he was working something over in his mind. Julie felt so shitty that she just let him sit there. Finally, he spoke again. "I know why it didn't kill me. It knew that doing so would cause more issues than it solved. But the fact that it didn't kill Nataliya is more concerning."

"How do you figure that?"

"You don't know as much about me as you think you do," he said. She might have been offended at his proclamation if she weren't in abject misery. "But it also knew what it would do to me if Nataliya were hurt. The fact that it only knocked her over is strange."

"Do you think that's significant?"

"Possibly. The rapes were all spaced apart. Then it killed four people and two dogs in one go. Maybe it needs to recharge from expending all that energy, and it couldn't kill Nataliya because it was depleted. I don't know the finer details about how a rabisu operates, but either way, it didn't do anything unusual for a regular man. It wasn't superhumanly strong, and it broke Nataliya's phone and ran off before she could call 911. It could be that Brian Peralta's sensibilities were winning over, or it could actually be vulnerable. Or both. I don't know."

"If it's vulnerable, that's a good thing."

"It's also a good thing if Peralta has some control," Patrick said. "Humans, even depraved ones, can be spoken to."

"I've seen enough depravity that I know that's not always true, Patrick. Not everyone can be lured by their weakness."

"That's not exactly what I meant." He shrugged. "But I understand what you're saying. I just hope it doesn't kill again before I get out of here. And it will kill again. The problem is that if Brian dies, it will have no problems jumping to another host. It can't be killed just by killing the host."

"So how do we get rid of it?" Julie leaned forward on the chair, pushing her glasses on top of her head. She'd acclimated to the lights a bit, but he winced nevertheless.

Patrick let out a sigh. "And that's the problem. I don't know."

"Alrighty. Great talk. So we aren't any closer than we were before." Julie flopped back.

"I wouldn't say that. Each time it attacked me and it wasn't able to do much. The first time was in its true form, and it burned my arms. They've healed already. As far as I can tell, the rabisu was burned just as badly as I was. It didn't expect that touching me would have such a devastating consequence. The second time, last night, it was using Peralta's body. It could only hurt me by mundane means. It knows it's not going to be able to destroy me like it did the others. If anyone has a shot at getting rid of this thing, it's me."

"What makes you so special, then?"

Patrick chuckled. "Do you think I'm going to give that to you so easily? Do me a favor. Get in contact with Liv. Tell her the verbena might have worked, but the bauble didn't hide me from the rabisu. Tell her I need Charon's obol. She'll know what you're talking about."

"Can't you get it from her?"

Patrick shook his head then let out a grunt. She supposed his head was still pretty tender. "Phone's dead," he said and touched the edge of the bandage. "Nataliya is at my house getting my charger and laptop.

It'll be a bit before she gets back. Besides, Liv knows you. She'll make sure to put this on priority."

Julie wasn't too sure about that, but she had a feeling the favor was because of Patrick's reluctance to have Liv actually speak to Nataliya in any way. But she wasn't about to say that. "Fine, fine. I'm hungover, but I'll do it for you," she said.

"Thanks."

"You know, I'm surprised you still have Nataliya this close to you, running errands. After all, the rabisu threatened her."

Patrick shrugged. "It's not my decision," he replied, his voice weary. "And I can only do so much to protect her. I'd prefer for her to concentrate on me right now, and not on the rabisu."

Ah. Well, that made more sense than him not wanting Liv to glimpse his lady love. "Sure thing. I'll come back as soon as I can." She stood up and slid her sunglasses back over her eyes.

"Have an egg bagel sandwich," Patrick said. "They got me through some ill-advised weekends in undergrad."

Julie wrinkled her nose. She didn't want to imagine strait-laced Dr. Morana engaging in binge drinking as a sprightly young man. But too late, her mind was already working much faster on such a mental picture than on the case at hand. She hurried out of the room before her imagination went wild.

Liv sent him a potted plant. It was verbena. The hospital volunteer had dropped it off, along with a thick manila envelope, right after lunch time. The purple flowers livened up the drab room. He opened the envelope and pulled out a handwritten letter, along with a small and flat tissue-wrapped package.

Dear Patrick,

I am rather flabbergasted that the charm didn't hide you. It should have. As soon as you are out of the hospital, please come see me and we can find out what is wrong with it. I'm sorry to hear about your injury and I'm glad you were able to get into surgery right away. Agent Lyons explained to me what happened, though I'm sure some of it was muddled due to her obvious hangover.

Enclosed is Charon's Obol. I don't expect I'll get this one back. You're going to have to repay me for this one. It's 5th century B.C. Don't worry, it's not worth nearly as much as the charmed amulet.

You're going to have to explain to me how a 4th century B.C. Greek coin relates to a 2,000 B.C. Akkadian demon, but I figure that's a story for when you're not lying injured in a hospital. You certainly have made larger logical leaps in the past, but I'm still completely confused. You keep your secrets close, Patrick. I can appreciate that, even as I'm dying of curiosity.

Just don't do anything foolish, okay? You've helped me a lot, and I don't want to lose you. You've brought me too much business. All kidding aside, I'm scared. I'm too used to you sitting in your morgue, doing autopsies, and staying away from the danger. Leave the danger to the professionals, okay?

I know nothing I say will stop you, so just take this verbena and be safe.

-Liv

Patrick put down the letter, knowing full well he wasn't going to take her advice. He tore the tissue paper off the parcel. Charon's obol, a bronze coin stamped with a bee design, rested on a folded piece of dark blue fabric. He put the coin on his side table and unfolded the fabric. It was embroidered with tiny, delicate stitches in white thread. The stitches formed the design of a key, with Greek letters above it forming a single word. Patrick's Greek was much rustier than his Latin, but he knew enough to muddle through some old texts. This word he knew well. Τάρταρος. Tartarus.

He closed his eyes, a sense of hope flooding through him. Liv had come through in a big way. He really, really owed her this time.

As he regarded the fabric, he heard a knock on the door.

"Come in," he said.

Nataliya came in, carrying a tote bag and wrapped up in a heavy coat. "It's getting cold," she said. She set the tote bag on his swivel table. It was from the Art Museum, and it read "Museum Nerd" in retro font. "You have a shocking dearth of tote bags," she said with a lopsided smile. "What do you use for groceries?"

"You can lecture me about saving the world from plastic bags later," he said, wishing he was in the mood for the banter. "Can I have my charger please?"

"Of course." Nataliya took his somber tone in stride. She plugged in the charger behind his hospital bed, then she draped the cord over the bedside and handed him the phone. He plugged it in and turned it on. "Do you need anything else?" she asked.

Patrick didn't know if he did or not. He bit his lip. "Just stay here for a bit, please?"

"Of course," she repeated. She sat down on one of the chairs and watched as he waited for his phone to boot up and connect to 5G.

He looked up at her and met her eyes. "Natashenka, I need to tell you something."

All traces of humor were gone. "What's wrong, Patrick?"

"I'm going to do something extremely dangerous, and I can't let you be a part of it. For your sake, and for your daughter's."

"What are you going to do?"

"I'm going to banish the rabisu, and Julie will help me. It'll be dangerous, especially since it's still attached to Brian Peralta."

"You've already been through emergency surgery," Nataliya said. "And you're going to put yourself through that?"

"I'm the only one who can," Patrick said. That wasn't entirely true, but it was close. He had to do this before the rabisu killed again, and there wasn't any time to find someone who had the skills necessary.

"How do you know that you won't die too?"

Patrick felt a smile tug at his lips. "I don't know that. But it's a risk I'm going to have to take. You know that this demon can't be allowed to run free. I have to do what I can. Come here."

Nataliya got up and went over to his bedside. He took her hand and squeezed it with his own. "Please, listen to me. I don't want you or your child to be hurt, and that means you have to stay away from this hospital. Go back to my house and stay there until I call the house phone."

"You still have a house phone?"

"Now is not the time."

Nataliya scoffed. "Well, if it matters to you, I care about you. This thing has already proven that it can hurt you in a way that matters."

Patrick smiled and squeezed her hand again. "I appreciate your concern. What can you do to help, though?"

She shrugged, a frown forming on her lips. "You're right, and I hate that you're right," she said. She looked down at their joined hands. "Patrick, I don't want you to put yourself in danger again, but I understand why you need to. I hope Julie isn't too hungover to help you."

"She'll be fine," Patrick replied with more conviction than he felt. He was sure Julie would be okay; she was a federal agent after all. But that didn't mean he was happy about her current state.

Nataliya nodded, an absent look on her face. "Do you know how long this will take?"

Patrick shook his head, then grimaced in pain. He hadn't learned when Julie was there earlier. "I wish I could tell you. This thing is locked onto me, but I don't know what kind of victims it wants since Peralta's family is all dead."

Nataliya pulled her hand away and went over to the museum bag. She rummaged around in it before pulling out a fabric zipper bag. She unzipped it and pulled out something shiny.

"What's that?" he asked, keeping his eyes on her. He still had a hard time focusing his vision, especially on things at a distance.

"Something my *babushka* gave me when I went to Russia after graduating from high school. I was fifteen." She walked back to his bedside and handed him a lacquered bangle. "It's too big for my wrist, but I carried it with me all throughout college, med school, and my residency. She said that it survived the Revolution, and she knew she could never sell it. Not even when she was starving with my *dedushka*. I think it will bring you the peace it brought me. And the courage of my family who survived the Imperial days, the Revolution, and the decades of communism."

Patrick looked at the thin bangle. He put it on the hand without the IV. It fit well. It was painted with the Firebird in reds and oranges against a black background.

"I won't insult you by refusing such a valuable item. I'll return it when this is all over."

Nataliya bit her lip. "No, keep it. It fits your wrist better."

Patrick looked at the bangle. "Fine. But I'm giving it back to your daughter when she turns fifteen. It belongs in your family, Natashenka."

She smiled at that. "Again, so sure the baby is a girl?"

"Yes."

She leaned forward and hugged him a bit awkwardly. He managed to sit up enough to return the hug. Her warmth was comforting. He didn't want to let go of that warmth, of her breath and her vitality. "Be safe," she said. "*Solnyshka moya.*"

Instead of letting go, Patrick cradled her face and kissed her. She returned the kiss with passion, and he felt like he was going to lose himself for the love of her. He hadn't kissed anyone like that before, and he was happy that it had been her.

When she pulled away, she smiled at him. "About time you did that," she said. She mumbled something in Russian and turned away. Her cheeks were nearly as red as her hair.

"Goodbye, *solnyshka moya*," she said.

She left without another word. He wondered what the Russian phrase meant, but he didn't dwell on it. He already missed her warmth.

CHAPTER TWENTY-ONE

Julie walked into the hospital room, feeling marginally better after a shower and a smoothie with some special additions. She wasn't sure if she wanted to know what those additions were. The smoothie shop by her apartment had obviously seen more than a few hangovers that day and were advertising a special smoothie for those who had indulged a bit too much New Year's cheer. It tasted rank, but it did help.

"Good, you're here," Patrick said as soon as he saw her. "Nataliya left a little while ago. I need your help. Have you heard from Beck?"

"Asshole is still out cold. I went to check on him to make sure he's still alive."

"Okay."

Julie walked to his bedside and looked at what he had spread out on his lap. A square of embroidered dark blue fabric. An old coin lay on top of it. Verbena flowers were strewn about on the bed covers. He had the necklace from Liv around his neck, and a red and black bangle on his wrist. The jewelry looked odd against his hospital gown and partially shaved and stitched head.

"Can you get me a cup of water?"

Julie did as he asked, grabbing the water cup with his hospital room number written on it. She went into the bathroom to use the tap. "Here," she said when she was finished.

Patrick took it in hand. "Once the rabisu shows up, you need to block the door. The last thing I need is a nurse doing her rounds to get caught up in this."

"How do I do that?" Julie asked. Hospital rooms were designed to prevent that very thing from happening.

"You're the fed," Patrick replied in a dry tone. "You should have some training in blockading an entrance."

Julie rolled her eyes. She'd use her own body if she had to.

Patrick dipped his fingers into the water, then he made the sign of the cross.

"That's not holy water, you know," Julie stated.

He didn't reply. He dipped his fingers in it again and wiped it over both eyelids. He started chanting in a strange language. After a moment, he spoke in English. "Are you ready? Last chance to back out."

"I'm ready," Julie said, feeling more confident than she had in days.

Patrick set the cup aside and lifted the coin, using the cloth as a barrier between the bronze and his fingers. "Once I summon him, it could take minutes to hours, depending on how far away he is. Do not let your guard down."

Julie nodded. She was trained for all sorts of situations, and Patrick knew it. It also helped that she had some concept of what they were up against, unlike Beck and the others in her St. Louis office. She stood in the doorway, watching the quiet hallway. Behind her, Patrick spoke again in that strange language. She felt a weird shift in her awareness, almost like the room was tilting. Or maybe it was like gravity was shifting around her, pulling at her from a different angle. It was disorienting, and she put a hand on the doorway to steady herself.

She willed her body to adapt, even as the shift became more pronounced. Patrick fell silent. Julie was shocked when she looked at the clock on the wall. The minute hand moved almost as fast as the second hand.

Then, it stopped. A nurse, who came into view at that moment, froze in time. Julie tried to breathe, but her body wouldn't move. It felt like a suffocating eternity before time snapped back. The nurse walked past. The clock ran as normal, and Brian Peralta appeared in front of her.

"Move," he said.

She moved. Once he strode past her, she shut the door and grabbed the handle. She should have grabbed something to brace the door, but it was too late now. Julie twisted around to see Brian advancing to Patrick's bed.

"You're an idiot," Peralta said, sweeping his arms out. "I'll kill you and the woman."

Julie pushed back against the door and unholstered her gun.

"You won't kill me," Patrick said. He pushed himself to a higher seat, though Julie thought he looked far too pale to be boasting to the possessed man. "I am the Verum Mortem, and you do not belong among the living."

Verum Mortem? Mortem meant death but she couldn't remember what verum meant.

Peralta lunged and stopped short of touching Patrick. He skidded backward a step, his arms flailing. Patrick held up the obol. He spoke in a language that Julie couldn't understand. She wasn't sure if it was the same one as earlier.

"Stop! No!" Brian spat out, then hissed wordlessly. He writhed and fell to the ground. Sounds came from deep in his throat. He punched at the air several times before he grabbed the side-bar of the bed. Peralta screamed.

"Shoot him, Julie. Now!"

Julie, startled at the command, obeyed without a second thought. She shot Peralta in the back of the head. Blood splattered on the white bedsheets and onto Patrick. At the crack of the gunshot, a monstrous creature materialized on Peralta's shoulders and let out an earsplitting shriek. Julie gasped as it rose from Peralta's prone body and tried to fly toward her. But Patrick held it back. The fabric that had wrapped the obol was now wrapped around the rabisu's leg, protecting Patrick's hand. He'd grabbed it when Peralta was falling to the ground.

Patrick spoke in that strange language again, sweat running down his face and causing the blood splatter to run.

Someone tried to open the door, and Julie pushed harder against it. Her gun was still drawn. Gravity shifted as before.

The rabisu froze in the air, and Patrick's muscles visibly tensed. For a moment, it looked like gravity shifted sideways, and Julie's hair floated around her, drops of blood and sweat rising into the air. Then, the droplets froze. It was as if time had stopped, but her mind didn't. She blinked, trying to make sense of it. A strange aura appeared in her vision, like the beginning of a migraine. It unfolded, then disappeared, leaving a very tall figure in its place. It was an old, thin man with a long unkempt beard. He wore loose robes, his sickly pale chest mostly bare. He slid his gaze past Julie and her breath stopped at his eyes. They were made of flames. She couldn't move as he turned to look at Patrick.

"You have called me," he said, his voice crooning. There was an underlying voice speaking at the same time, an octave lower and in another language. "Taking me away from my boat is a dangerous thing."

"Take this ancient creature and cast him into Tartarus," Patrick said, holding out the obol. "In the name of Thanatos."

The figure let out a low rumble. "The trickster son of death. I know you." With one hand he took the coin, and with the other he grabbed the rabisu by the neck. The creature had stopped struggling when the man appeared, and now it let out a high-pitched whine of fear. "You pay the toll to Charon. I will accept this price. Do not expect me to do this favor again, son of Verum Mortem." He put the coin in the folds of his flowing robes and reached forward to take Patrick's throat in his hand. "For I will take you back and claim you as my servant."

Patrick gasped and tried to beat back Charon's hand. "It's not my time! You can't take me!" His voice was a mere whisper as Charon strangled him.

Julie struggled against the frozen time. She had to help Patrick. She slowly, so slowly, raised the gun in the air. What good would a bullet do against the Ferryman? She had to try. She squeezed the trigger, aiming for Charon's back. The bullet struck, and Charon staggered and let go of both the rabisu and Patrick. The rabisu shrieked and dove for Julie.

Charon grabbed the rabisu before it could touch her. "You have a stupid courage, mortal woman," Charon said, those fiery eyes fixed on her. "But you are right. Thanatos would be displeased if I took him, even if I wanted him more than an end to my torment." Charon stuck his hand into his own chest, though there was no blood. He pulled his hand back out, holding the bullet in between his skeletal fingers. "For you, as a reminder that your foolish courage saved you. Because you amused the Ferryman. You won't always be so lucky."

Without thinking, Julie took the bullet in her own hand. As soon as she did, Charon disappeared with the rabisu, leaving a flash of the aura in his wake. Julie's entire awareness jolted, like a puzzle piece snapping into place.

She collapsed to the ground, half out of her own head. A mere moment later, the door burst open, slamming against her side, and Julie was lost in a haze of the hospital personnel, security, and her own scramble of thoughts pinging around in her aching skull.

Nataliya ran into Patrick's hospital room. The new one. He'd explained to her that his original room was now a crime scene and he'd had to move to a different room down the hall because of it. A police officer stood at his bedside with a notebook and pen. Beck, wearing civilian clothes, sat on the guest chair and nursed a cup of coffee. He looked like hell. Deep, dark circles stood out under his eyes, which were bloodshot. His hair was mussed up and not in a carefree way.

"That's all we need, Dr. Morana," the cop said. "Based on Agent Lyons's testimony, and yours, this was a clear-cut case of self-defense. Thank you."

Patrick nodded as the officer left the room. His face was splattered with blood, though some of it was smeared.

"Y'all had fun without me," Beck said.

"You're barely coherent as it is," Patrick retorted. "And Nataliya wasn't here either."

Nataliya ignored the conversation and hurried over to Patrick's bedside. "What happened?" she asked, her voice tight. "There's blood on your face."

Patrick lifted his fingers and brushed his cheek, completely missing the splatter on the other temple. "Oh," he said. "Yeah, I changed into a new gown too but I guess I forgot to wash my face. Julie killed Peralta."

Nataliya knew there was much more to it than he was letting on, but with Beck in the room he wasn't going to spill the details. She didn't ask. "I guess that's not the worst bodily fluid you've gotten on yourself," she muttered. She saw a pile of alcohol wipes on the side table, so she opened one and helped Patrick wipe his face.

"Hey, why weren't you here?" Beck asked, as if just realizing what Patrick had said a few moments earlier.

"Patrick sent me home," Nataliya replied. "He said he wanted some rest." The lie slid easily off her tongue, and she almost felt guilty about it. However, she had a feeling that Beck wouldn't remember the conversation five minutes from now. She opened another wipe and finished cleaning Patrick's face. He gave her a soft smile when she was done.

"Why wasn't I here?" Beck asked.

"Because you were passed out so hard that Julie couldn't rouse you," Patrick retorted. "Do I need to write it out so a kindergartner could understand it?"

Beck glared. "I just hate missing things."

"Then maybe don't try to drink yourself into alcohol poisoning next time, hm?" Patrick shook his head. "Beck, you should really go home and get some rest."

"He's right," Nataliya said. She tossed the wipes and wrappers in the trash can. "Unless you want me to find a nurse to give you a fluid IV."

Beck jumped to his feet, the word IV triggering his fight-or-flight response. "Get well soon, Patrick, bye." He scampered out of the room.

Nataliya chuckled to herself as she watched him go. She crossed into the bathroom to wash her hands.

"How did you know that Beck is scared of IVs?" Patrick asked her when she came back out.

"He is?" Nataliya blinked. She hadn't known that but had been pleasantly surprised at his hasty exit. "Oh well, it doesn't matter. I'm glad you're all right. Did you. . . ?" She trailed off, wondering how to ask what she actually wanted to know.

"I got rid of the rabisu," Patrick confirmed. "I had to call in a favor. Sort of. It's complicated."

"A favor from whom?"

"Liv. She got me something that was pretty valuable, and I can't afford to repay her, so I have no idea what I'm going to do."

Nataliya threw her coat and purse onto the visitor's chair. "But you did it and you're alive," she said.

"Yeah," Patrick said with a half-smile. "Thanks to Julie's itchy trigger finger."

"She shot Peralta," Nataliya said to herself, wondering what had caused that to happen.

"Well, yeah, but that's not exactly what I was referring to. I'll tell you everything, but give me a moment, okay? I haven't had a moment to just be still since you left."

Nataliya didn't need to be told twice. She went to his bedside and sat down on the mattress. "I'm so thankful you're alive, Patrick. I was so afraid, and my mind went into some dark places."

He didn't say anything, just stared up at her with his vibrant green eyes. She still remembered the first day she met Patrick. After she'd ducked under that police tape at the crime scene, she'd straightened to meet the coroner's eyes. Large eyes, green as imperial jade, and completely thunderstruck. She was used to receiving admiring looks, but Dr. Patrick Morana had looked at her as if he had never seen something so precious. She could say it. It wasn't self-absorbed for her to admit that's how he was looking at her. He said it as much himself not a few hours ago. She was precious to him. And he was precious to her.

"Natashenka. I want you to know something," Patrick said, breaking into her thoughts.

"What is it?" she asked.

"I love you."

Her eyes widened. "You love me?" she asked.

"Yes. I don't know exactly what romantic love feels like. Maybe I just love you as a dear friend, a colleague, or maybe as a woman. But I love you. I want to protect you.

Patrick reached forward to take her hand, but she instead lay down on the bed next to him, tucked in just right. Patrick seemed to relax at her warmth, and she closed her eyes as they lay together in silence. That first meeting, he'd looked at her as if he didn't know what to do with this precious creature in front of him. She was too young to be the doctor who was accepted for the fellowship, perhaps, or maybe he didn't want the awkwardness of a hot colleague. Whatever it was, it had passed by quickly enough, leaving strict professionalism in place. But always that note of kindness, that sense that he was holding something very precious.

She smiled to herself and moved to whisper in his ear.

"I love you too, Patrick."

ACKNOWLEDGEMENTS

First and foremost, thank you to my parents, Jim and Mary Kruta, for always supporting my creative endeavors. You gave me an amazing example of how to be a good person, how to work hard, and how to have a good sense of humor. Second in this family list are my siblings Sander, Laura, Jim, and Paul. I couldn't have asked for a better family to grow up in. CORN! Third are all my nieces, nephews, grandnieces, and grandnephews. There are too many of you to list, but you all give me life and laughter. Little Jimmy especially, as he loves my cooking and drove me around when I injured my shoulder. I can't forget my sisters-in-law Valleri, Ginny, and Wendi for being as close as real sisters, and my brother-in-law Doug for being as close as a real brother.

Next, I must thank the friends who listened to me endlessly prattle on about writing. Special attention goes to Sebrina Eden, who helped me through the process of self-publishing. Swapping memes and snippets of our respective books kept me sane through my darkest times. I can't read to read book 2 of the Faultlines series. I'd also like to thank the other two members of the Triumvirate of Sin, Adam and Tiesha Klostermann, for going to see the hyenas with the zoo with me. Special shout outs to Dave Singleton for the many, many fun hours of D&D, Raf Richards for sushi dates, Erica Kosterman for always reading my fanfiction since we were little teenagers, Brandy Roosevelt for encouraging my fantasy reading habit since I was a kid, and to the members of the Gwethil for the support and love. Finally, I have to thank Bethany Wagner for not only being the best travel buddy, but being a source of inspiration, laughter, friendship, and Pride and Prejudice jokes.

I also need to thank the fluffy ones in my life. I spent many hours writing with Eisley the cat and Appa the Jack Chi on my lap. Cheddar the kitten came in late in the process, but he was definitely trying to mess with the keyboard as I formatted this book. Any faults in this

I blame retroactively on him. And of course, Anubis, the giant black beast with the booming bark and the sweetest personality.

My editor, Kyra Rodgers, did amazing work whipping this book into shape and letting the characters shine. Cover artist Jovanna Plata created a jaw dropping illustration for this book. She crawled inside my brain for my vision of Patrick and Nataliya. Thank you to Madelyn Rose Craig for helping me learn how to format the cover and sharing her resources.

Last but not least, I'd like to thank everyone who took a chance on me and picked up this book. You're my hero.

Soli Deo Gloria.

ABOUT THE AUTHOR

Catherine Kruta grew up in a family bakery and has a Bachelor's of Science in Geography. She has been writing since she was even shorter than she is now. A world traveler that has been to 6 continents, she has more hobbies than she knows what to do with. An avid swing dancer and equestrian, she loves the outdoors but doesn't believe in eating mushrooms.

Catherine lives in southern Illinois with 2 cats, 2 dogs, a snake, and her nephew.